Reunion

By R.J. Goldberg

Bethesda Communications Group

Published by the Bethesda Communications Group
Glen Echo, MD 20812
www.bcgpub.com

This is a work of fiction, and while certain places mentioned here may exist, all characters and events are entirely fictional. Any resemblance to actual persons or events is coincidental.

The photograph on the front cover is from Cornell University, and the photograph on the back cover is from the Lab School of the University of Chicago, both circa 1960.

ISBN-13: 978-0-9761364-9-1
ISBN-10: 0-9761364-9-X

This novel dedicated to:

Anita

Kathy and Kobi
Roger and Elena
Daniel and Betsy,
and
Maya, Sarah Ella, Jack, Lucia, Levi, Charlie, Carlo, Dante, Yonatan, Sofia and Nate,

and
in memory of my mother, Belle Malter Goldberg

Reunion

Book One
Michael

1

HE WAS OFTEN in the sun parlor on the phone or doing his homework, or, when he was just a little guy, peering over the window sill at dinner time to keep watch for his father's car. Their brick six-flat, like most of those buildings, ran deep and narrow, almost abutting the structures to either side of it. And thus the draw of the sun parlor, this window to the world where Michael could view the street below and the buildings opposite and beyond, and even a sliver of the lake. Uniquely Chicago to the east—the lake.

But you'd never hear mention of the east side of Chicago. You lived on the north side or the west side or, as the Steins did, on the south side where Michael's father, Sam Stein, on this particular evening, was packing the car to take him to upper New York the next day to begin his freshman year at Cornell. Traipsing up and down the stairs to and from their second floor apartment, Sam was careful to not disturb the Shuberts above them or the Lebovskis below them. He wouldn't want to stir their neighbors to pound on the floor or ceiling; that would be embarrassing.

"I want you to bed at a decent hour," he had directed Michael earlier that afternoon. "I'm going to be up late packing, and we've got a lot of driving to do. I want you to be able to spell me in the afternoon after lunch when I get tired. So please, no night owl stuff. You say goodbye to your friends, and get back here before midnight. You'll be seeing everyone again before you know it."

"How about 1:00?"

"No. You be home by 11:30. We're leaving at five in the morning."

Michael grimaced, though he knew deep-down his father was right.

"We're not stopping. We will, of course, for gas and to pee. But that's it. Hazel's going to make sandwiches, and we'll have pickles and candy bars. We're going straight through."

Which put him in a good mood again, his father's amusing combinations—pickles and no stops. And, in fact, they did get started on time that next morning at 5:00 a.m. and, driving straight through, were at a motel in Ithaca by 7:00 p.m.

"If you're checking for bedbugs, you pull the sheets *all* the way back!" Sam had chosen this drab, roadside motel so he wouldn't have to unload the trunk he had packed so painstakingly. At this modest little place he could see his car right outside the window.

"I'm doing that," Michael responded, though he really wasn't because he hated making such a mess of the bed.

"No, you're not!" his father replied. "Look, like this, *all* the way back."

Sam yanked the sheet and covers down with authority

as if it were a lesson for succeeding generations.

"That's the way you do it! Okay? Now you see, there's nothing. You stay here. I'm going to give her the money so we can leave first thing in the morning."

He left and was back a few minutes later, looking satisfied that he was running the trains on time. They ate the extra sandwiches Hazel had packed for dinner, Michael on his bed and his father on a chair, watching the Ed Sullivan Show, four young singers from England with a funny name, the Beatles. Their sound was good, Michael proclaimed prophetically, and then conked out for the night, he and his father in twin beds the last time they'd share a hotel room.

———————

The next morning, bright and early, they were up the hill at Cornell, the big parking lot outside the freshmen boys' dorms teeming with families like a refugee center.

"Give me that duffel! I've still got an arm free."

Sam was an ox when it came to hauling, which Michael found embarrassing, that this was the Ivy League and here he was—the son of a piano mover. Which wasn't really the case (though, no shame if it were). Sam had a plumbing supplies business and since he never professed to love it, Michael wondered why he was always in such a hurry to get back to it. He would leave for work each morning before Michael awakened for school, and he'd come home late in the evening after Michael and Elaine had finished dinner, a work ethic he had gotten, apparently, from *his* father. True to form on this first college morning, no sooner had they emptied the trunk of the car into his dorm room, Sam was reaching for his jacket and cap to go. And it wasn't yet 8:00 a.m.

"Well Son, we did it."

"We did it, yes," Michael replied, his cheeriness oozing away.

"I'm going to hit the road. I'll get a coffee on the way," Sam said, scraping the soles of his shoes uneasily against the floor. "But you get something to eat. The cafeteria over there is open." Sam gave him a $20 bill and pointed to a small annex structure clad with the same red brick as the dorms.

"You want to leave *now*, Dad?" Michael asked, though he couldn't picture his father helping him unpack, fold underwear, hang posters, organize his desk and dresser drawers. Not *his* father.

"If I don't, I won't make it past Michigan. You know how tough night driving is for me."

Sam would complain about the haloing of headlights. But, on the other hand, he had driven quite competently the night before for two hours in pitch black. Bottom line, Michael knew, was that when his father made up his mind to leave, you couldn't change it.

"I get it," he said, an imitation of his older sister, Elaine. She would use that expression when she knew their father had made up his mind.

They shook hands. He never got a hug, much less a kiss, though he envied the affection his father lavished on Elaine. "I'll write," he said, wiping away a tear. And somehow, at that moment, his father's controlling ways seemed okay.

"You call me on Sundays. Make it collect, you hear? Every Sunday! I want to know how you're doing."

"You got it," Michael replied. "I get it and you got it."

They laughed, which Sam took as his cue to exit. "We'll talk Sunday," he muttered, leaving the dorm room without so much as a look back.

"He's a vaudeville star!" a voice cackled with laughter behind the closed door of the next room.

And then the object of this mirth appeared, a 3-year old boy with a skimmer over his eyes, walking down the hall bumping into walls.

"He's going to hurt himself, Bill!" The mother ran to retrieve her toddler, not wanting the silliness to end badly.

It only made matters worse, Michael pined, these thin cement block walls where you could hear, three or four rooms down, the laughter that highlighted his own loneliness. And though a couple of boys wandered in mistaking his room for theirs, it was a full two hours before the right boy strode in with the certainty of belonging and, with no hesitation, slipped a duffel off each shoulder, the bags tumbling to the floor with a thud.

"Mike?" the boy asked.

"Michael Stein!" he responded, leaping from his chair, his arm extended for a handshake. He couldn't have kids calling him "Mike."

"Harold?"

"Hal!" the boy replied, in his case preferring the diminutive. At six feet, he was the taller by a few inches, and his hair and complexion lighter, though an outsider would have noted the resemblance between them with their square faces and regular features.

They stood for about 15 minutes in that same spot covering a range of subjects, mostly practical—like the room, their preferences as to space and sides—but within minutes were discussing sports, politics and girls.

"Are you hungry?" he asked Hal. He had been up for hours with only a small orange juice from a canteen at the motel.

"Starved! We can go *there*." Hal pointed to a cafeteria about fifty yards away. That was the good news—the proximity. The bad news, Michael would learn, was the quality.

"This is not what you had in mind, is it, man?" Hal asked, viewing Michael's poorly concealed grimace at the sole breakfast offering—a gooey omelet.

"Not really. Should we go somewhere else? I'm fine with just cereal."

"Hang on! I have that!" said a woman behind the counter. She ducked into the kitchen, reappearing a moment later with two small Cheerios boxes and a banana.

"I owe you my life!" Michael said with feigned drama.

As she ladled out the eggs and ham to Hal (he was good with gooey), Michael's thoughts turned to Hazel who would always have breakfast cereal for him, though she'd cut him no slack for any other meal. "Just shovel it down, boy!" she'd say in her Louisiana drawl. "It'll all be mush in yo stomach. You can be sho'a that."

And having lucked out with cereal, shovel it down he did that first cool September morning with his new roommate, Hal Hartfield.

2

SAM STEIN'S WIFE, Ruth, was only 39 when she died. As a single parent with two kids—Elaine, 10, and Michael, 6—Sam needed a live-in housekeeper. Eligibility requirements consisted of honesty (though not free from suspicion), single marital status, and basic cooking, cleaning and ironing skills. The longest lasting of these was Hazel Foreman, who had been their cleaning lady when Ruth was dying, and was pressed into service as the housekeeper. She met those basic requirements, and clinched the deal when she offered a seven-day workweek, which for her was no sacrifice, her obesity making a commute impractical.

During Hazel's regime, *everything* was brought in. Dave, the butcher's deliveryman who was a friend or relative of Hazel's (Michael never knew) would bound up the back stairs two steps at a time, singing "Poolah! Hey Poolah! You dere, Baby? I gotcha you some'm good today."

And she'd respond, always the same way.

"Yeah, Dave. Where you think I be."

And after she took the package of meat from him and

turned around, he'd slap her huge behind.

"Y'g'on now, Dave," she'd say, as if she were chiding him, "and make yo' other deliveries before I call the *po'*-lice."

He'd laugh, and then she'd laugh too.

The milkman, as well as the grocer's and dry-cleaner's deliverymen, came up this same outdoor wooden stairway that abutted the back of the building and fanned out to the porch landing. It was down these stairs that Michael accessed the back yard, a small square of lawn between their six-flat and the garages lining the alleyway. This back alley, hosting the garbage cans, was peppered with bottle tops and other collectibles that crunched under the wheels of the milk, coal and peddler wagons.

"Rags for Sale!" the peddler would chant, and if he or the guy sharpening knives stopped their rigs in the alley, as they would occasionally for lunch, you could hear a horse chomping on the food in the feedbag, and smell some newly minted manure, these sounds and smells accompanied, on a windy day, by the flapping of the sheets and towels on the laundry line straining to escape the clothespins.

"One more inning?" he would ask, a beggar when it came to Sox games.

"I'll inning *you*, Boy," she'd reply, the expert at turning nouns into verbs.

There'd be no schedule changes when it came to bedtime. The radio was off by 9:00 P.M, and no amount of pleading could change that, a rule Hazel applied without hypocrisy. After it was turned off, she wouldn't turn it on for herself, though the truth was she'd be dying to know the score.

She'd switch to the little black and white TV in her room and wrestling (which she liked even more than baseball), and she'd watch that until midnight, the only real match being Hazel and the wire antenna she'd bend and twist to view her beloved fakery more clearly. It was the script and the way the wrestlers stuck to it that made the illusion so compelling. George was always Gorgeous and Chief Don Eagle always savage, which gave Hazel's life a consistency that reality never could.

"I'll be going then, Mr. Stein," she would reluctantly announce each Sunday since Sam had declared it a compulsory day off.

That wasn't his idea. He had valued that seven-day workweek, indeed it was one of Hazel's principal attractions. Over time, however, his girlfriend Maude had the desire to look wifely, and that would entail donning an apron (it looked like an evening gown) and cooking Sam some grub (definitely grubby). And so she cajoled him into a compulsory day off for Hazel, and hence this new weekly ritual of Hazel standing at the front door on Sunday mornings with a large canvas bag, sweat trickling from the top of her forehead down the folds of her neck, a sign to Sam of guilt (he never did understand obesity).

"All right, Hazel," he'd reply, refusing to look up, convinced this large bag she held was stuffed with food for her relatives.

No reprieve in sight, she'd waddle laboriously out the front door, though immobility wasn't her chief concern. She feared the black-on-black violence of the west side where she would be going to spend her day at a cousin's. She'd take a couple of buses followed by a walk, treacherous in broad daylight, from her last stop to her cousin's place (Sam paid for a cab back in the evening). That was the routine until Michael left for college, at which time his family moved back to Hyde Park to a tower building with an unobstructed view of the lake. And as for Hazel, who Sam had decided was a fit for the flat but not for the tower, he gave her two weeks' pay and, in his words, let her go.

———————

"What would you think," his father had asked him a week before they left for Cornell, "if I let Hazel go after I take you up to school?"

He was packing when his father introduced this subject, packing all the clothes Hazel had so neatly washed, pressed and folded. It seemed that everything he did these days had to do with college. Now Hazel's job did too, apparently. Because he would be leaving, so would she.

"What's this all about?" he asked.

"I don't really need her, Son." His father was sitting at the end of the bed. "With you gone, I'll be going out more. What I'll need is a cleaning lady once a week. But a housekeeper? That's an indulgence. Our rent in Hyde Park will be more than double this rent here." He paused. "And I'll have your tuition, room and board and travel costs. It's an indulgence."

He looked at his father with empathy. Cornell was expensive, and he wasn't on scholarship or loan or anything of the kind. And this was a man who himself had dropped out of college because his family couldn't afford it; they had all heard that story a thousand times. Did he have any right to insist on his keeping Hazel?

"I guess I hadn't thought it through, Dad." He felt an ache in his gut, like he was too young to be making these decisions. But he was the cause, wasn't he? Or his leaving was. Or was it the higher rent in the new tower building?

Or was it Hazel's obesity and his father's concern about image in their new location?

"I've talked to people," his father said, as if he had read his mind, "and there's cleaning help out there for a lot less than Hazel gets. So I'm not going to insult her and cut her down from seven days a week to one, and then less per day for even the one. I'm not going to do that. She'll find something else."

Which launched another flood of regrets. Because if there was one thing that he was aware of more than his father, it was that Hazel had been stuck in their house for a decade, and so what was she going to find? Who were her contacts? What was that "something else" going to be, when she could hardly make her way to an interview?

———————

He fidgeted with his spoon and empty juice carton, waiting for Hal to finish his eggs. He could only imagine what was happening in Chicago around now. Hazel would be boxing things for the move to Hyde Park. His father, in suit and tie and antsy to get to the office, would inform her of his long-term plans. He'd be traveling more, he'd tell her, now that he was an empty nester or whatever they called parents whose children weren't around in the dark ages of firing people for being fat.

"I actually liked that dish." Hal said, carrying his tray to the disposal area.

Michael too disposed of his tray and then, with Hal, stepped outdoors into the cool air and bright sunlight to begin their steep ascent up Libe Slope to the bookstore to purchase course materials. This wide, verdant hill that separated the freshmen boys' dorms at the bottom from the signature buildings at the top, was just one of the vistas that made the campus so scenic. Walking and talking, undistracted by the running dogs and flying Frisbees, they traded information like espionage agents. Hal's father a philosophy professor, Columbia's department chair no less. And Hal's mother a Harrison of railroad fame and fortune, one of New York's most storied families. Hal had attended Grovener, a snooty prep school in Perkins, Pennsylvania (his preppy attire no accident).

"I'd like to do junior year abroad," he told Hal, tossing his French book into his basket. "Or at least a summer. I've never been out of the country, or anywhere else for that matter."

"For real?" Hal had a skeptical look, as if his new roommate were pulling his leg.

"Well, there was summer camp in Wisconsin. And I canoed for a week in the Boundary Waters on the Canadian border. But no, I've never traveled other than that, not even to New York."

"You're *in* New York, man. You're better traveled than you think. Anyways, traveling abroad is overrated. I've been to Europe a bunch of times, but there are too many places here I haven't seen. I'd love to do the Boundary Waters. I've heard it's cool."

They chatted like this for another hour while checking and double-checking the books they were buying against the course lists, and then, after their purchases were complete, began their descent down Libe Slope to the dorm. They were quiet now as if all talked out.

It was a lot to process, Michael mused. Hal's scholarly father and wealthy mother, the Harrison side of the family so well known that even he knew who they were, and he was a Chicago boy. As for Hal, he wasn't a dull rich kid; to the contrary, seemed interesting, smart and worldly. He had made several trips to Europe, and lived in France for a while, though not with his folks. It didn't sound like their family did much of anything together, except host dinner parties for professors and other scholars, university administrators, and think tank people from Washington. High powered stuff that Hal, it was apparent, took in stride.

That evening after dinner, they attended a fireworks display on Lake Cayuga. It had been a long day for Hal who had been up the night before, packing. No sooner had they returned to the dorm, he plopped onto the bed fully clothed, shoes and all.

"I don't have my valet," he said. "I'll have to sleep like this."

"You had a valet?" Michael asked, suspecting his gullibility was being tested.

"Of course not, you goof!" And a moment later he was sound asleep while Michael lay awake...remembering.

For six consecutive summers, beginning at age 8, he would take a night train to toss and turn in a cloth curtained berth of a Pullman sleeping car pounding the rails to the North Woods of Wisconsin for an eternity of eight weeks. The camp he went to had a kitschy Indian name but it wasn't down on the reservation, filled as it was with silver-spooned boys forming cliques the moment the train pulled away.

By his last years there he would hear his name chanted in the mess hall the morning of an inter-camp competition.

"Steino! Steino, He's our man! If he can't do it, nobody can!"

He was a player to be sure (on the camp's baseball team, that is), and you'd think this adulation would have immunized him from the doubts and disappointments of his teen years. But not so, because as he lay sleepless this first night in his dorm room, still technically a teenager, those cheers weren't even a whisper anymore. Only the more humbling camp experiences reverberated—the pee-soaked bedding when he was eight and nine, the "red-bellies" and "pink chests" by bullying older campers, his failed attempts to nap at rest-period, the infirmary confinements and, at mail time, the floridly penned letters the other boys received from their mothers.

Well, not all the other boys, in truth, not Joe DiMaggio Jr. the summer he was there. With his long face and Roman nose, he was a Yankee Clipper clone with rosy cheeks. It felt unreal to have the great DiMaggio's son there and in his cabin no less. And since it was only that one season, it would seem like a dream years later, the things he would ask Joe Jr.—"Did your Dad like Mickey Mantle? Was Yogi Berra really funny?"—though he never got much in the way of answers. Certainly not to the most masturbatory wondering of every camper of sufficient pubescence—whether Marilyn Monroe would be there on Visitors Day. By the time that day arrived, with speculation at a fever pitch, he could see that the camper at the center of it all, Joe Jr., had grown increasingly sullen.

When the gate to the long gravel road opened at the prescribed hour, the cars began their procession to the main parking lot, parents claiming their kids and moving on as the waiting throng thinned and disappeared.

"Looks like you put on a pound or two!" Sam said excitedly. He had come with his sister, Florence.

"I'm not sure about that," she said, it being apparent

to her that her nephew had already lost about half the ten pounds he would usually shed during the camp season.

He pumped his father's hand, hugged and kissed his aunt, and led them in the direction of the mess hall where the director had set up refreshments. In passing his own cabin, he saw a face inside turn slowly from the window. It was Joe Jr., tears streaming down those rosy cheeks. It was beyond sullenness, he realized, now that it was a certainty no one was coming, not the Yankee Clipper or his wife, Marilyn Monroe, and far more hurtful, not the first Mrs. DiMaggio, Joe Jr.'s mother. No, nobody was coming for Joe, the only boy in the camp on Visitors Day without a visitor.

———————

"If you learn nothing else in this class, you will know the War of the Roses is not a horticultural event."

And that opening-day line, it's sad to say, was about all you *could* learn from Professor Frederick Horton—Freddie's Class, as the students called it, an English History course derided as "castles without hassles." Hardly the norm on a campus paced by its Bronx Science and Stuyvesant alums, and known for its academic intensity, Horton's class was a notorious *gut* (in Cornell-speak, easy), his rambling lectures a naptime for the jocks in possession of his previous exams (complete with answers) that had circulated through their locker room.

"It's funny that we have almost the same classes," Michael had remarked to Hal when they were up at the bookstore buying their course materials.

And it was true that, except for Freddie's Class, their schedules were identical. Which was nuts because Hal was in beginning French, though he had spent some serious time in France and could speak the language with a convincing Parisian accent.

"Why exactly *are* you in 101?" Michael asked Hal once classes had been underway.

"Because it's not just speaking, that's why."

"But you read well also." Based on the classes Michael had already attended, it would take him years, he felt, to get to Hal's reading level.

"I can read decently, yes, but I can't write worth a damn. I never did learn grammar."

And that was the problem, that there were students (many of them) who enrolled in the entry-level course because they thought they had gaps or it would boost their grade average. A curse and a blessing for Michael, it would turn out, because his roommate was one of those ringers, and it was his coaching that saved him. As for Philosophy, he would get from Hal the kind of insights you could expect only from someone teaching the subject.

"What do *you* think, Mr. Hartfield?" Stuart Brin, their Philosophy professor, would address Hal in a 200-person lecture. "Does that sound like an oversimplification?" This deference remarkable to the other students, who would look around and wonder why this Hartfield kid had an opinion of interest to the department chair.

3

GIVEN THE SMALL size and intimacy of Michael's high school—U-High, grades 9 through 12 of the University of Chicago's Laboratory School—napping wasn't an option.

"I've been speaking gibberish! And not one of you has questioned it!" exclaimed Paul O'Hara, his third-year English teacher. He slammed his book down, the desk still shuddering.

"If you had done the reading and had been awake for the last fifteen minutes, you would have disagreed with every piece of rubbish I just uttered!"

O'Hara was a patient man. But this overly social and inattentive English class had tipped the balance. The cure he devised was to spout sheer nonsense, which he had just done for the past quarter-hour without a single voice raised to question or object.

"You decide, boys and girls," he continued, "what you want from this class, what you want from life for that matter, and whether you're here to learn or just exhaust the oxygen supply." His eyes scanned each of them, and then he picked up his book—Thomas Hardy's *Return of the Native*.

"I'll look for something better from you tomorrow. Class dismissed!"

O'Hara walked out. In stunned silence, they sat for another couple of minutes, and then filed out and down the corridor, through the main entrance of the building. This was their last class. It was early afternoon, but unusually dark, the rooms within the building illuminated and lively.

He trudged to the corner bus stop with his classmate Eddie and, within minutes, they boarded a bus that was nearly empty, not like the cattle car he normally would have taken an hour later.

"I can't believe it," he said.

"I know," said Eddie, unashamed of repeating the exact expression, "I can't believe it."

Two stops later the bus filled with older boys from St. Philip, the Catholic high school, who were on an earlier schedule.

"Keep your eyes on the floor!" he whispered to Eddie, viewing the black buckle shoes and white socks of the St. Philip kids, a fashion apart from the brown penny loafers and argyle stockings of the U-High boys.

Tense the whole time, the ride seemed longer than the usual ten minutes. When they arrived at their stop they were the only ones to get off, and as the bus pulled away they breathed a sigh of relief, though still walking briskly lest someone in black buckle shoes appear.

"I've got a lot of reading tonight." Michael was referring to the reading he should have done the evening before.

"I'm going to finish the book," Eddie said, which he

could easily do. He was a great reader, the least likely to have been busted by O'Hara's ruse.

After Eddie entered his building, Michael crossed the street to his own, and then slowly ascended the two flights of stairs as if he were going to his hanging. The moment he opened the door, he saw Hazel vacuuming, her expression upon seeing him one of shock. She yanked the plug out of the wall and didn't move, in basically a freeze position.

"Whach'you doin here at this hour, boy?" She never needed a watch.

He told her what happened and she listened without blinking an eye. And then when he had finished, she put the plug back and resumed the noisy vacuuming.

"I 'spect you learned something you don't learn in books," she said, her last couple of words barely audible over the loud whirr of the motor.

And that said it all, he reflected, because if Thomas Hardy hadn't made an impression, Paul O'Hara had. By senior year, there were the first stirrings of what you could call intellectuality, the primordial ooze of deeper thoughts, and study habits that went beyond the average effort for those teachers like Paul O'Hara he wouldn't disappoint. Without knowing it, he was ready for college.

4

IN THE FIRST few years after his wife's death, Sam would take the kids to the cemetery on Mother's Day to place plants on her grave. If he had a tendency, ordinarily, to be a compulsive talker, that was nothing compared to his nonstop mumblings in this disconsolate state.

"I have no idea why they gave me this. A bunch of conmen," he complained, inspecting the plant that was the subject of his dissatisfaction.

"This is more of a flower," he continued, barely within earshot of his two kids who were unwrapping other items from the florist. "It needs sun, and there's nothing but shade here. They know you're on your way to the cemetery. So they take advantage, the bastards."

It was at moments like these that Elaine pitied her father, his inability to manage his anger. She had grown up quickly in that period just before and after her mother's death, looking after her brother when their father was at the hospital. Now still only 12, she would try to stay in her own head, to remember how much fun Mother's Day used to be. The food and artwork she'd make for her mom who pretended they were the greatest of creations. And with those thoughts to console her, she would imagine her mom knew they were there, and so she'd arrange the plants just the way she would have wanted them.

"It's a flowering plant, Dad" Elaine responded. "It doesn't need much light. The lady told us that, you remember?"

He didn't, though he could never remember anything about plants or flowers. But it was good Elaine remembered, he said, and then the tears drenching his handkerchief, a white flag of surrender signifying it was time to leave. He had met Ruth Harris the summer before he started college, when she was working the checkout desk of the Hyde Park branch of the public library, She had only to make some intriguing comments about the books he had selected, and the rest was history. They were inseparable, and when she died, for a long time after, he was lost, frantic in everything he did and thought and said. And that's when he arranged to have her belongings shipped to his company's warehouse, because he couldn't look at them; an ill-fated decision, it turned out, because they were lost in a fire. The only items that survived were her gold watch and wedding ring (in a box at the bank), and a few items of no monetary value that had been in the hands of others: her recipes (on note-cards her sister had kept), crochet needles, a mahjong set, a small purse, a thimble from the incinerated sewing kit, a decorative demitasse and saucer she had given to a friend, some hairpins, a veil, and two scarves she had knitted before she died—one for her son and one for her daughter.

Three months after the funeral, Sam and his kids went to synagogue for High Holiday services. He would greet his fellow congregants with a "Happy New Year!" as if this could be taken literally. To all outward appearances, Michael and Elaine looked great in their new fall outfits, and he, as well, in a suit he had custom tailored for the holidays. But who were they kidding? They were the walking wounded.

"We're going to move to South Shore," Sam told his sister Florence.

"I thought you liked Hyde Park?" she replied.

"I do," he said, "but every street I walk is a street I walked with Ruth. I need some time and space...and space is the only thing I can control."

———

Their six-flat in South Shore was four blocks from the Isabelle O'Keefe School.

"Michael! Come up here!" his fifth grade teacher demanded. He had just passed a note across the aisle.

He peered down the long row that led to her pointy chin, then pulled his arm back to his side, the note stuck in his hand.

"Yes, Miss Mulroy."

He sat up straight, still hoping the storm might pass.

"Don't keep me waiting, Michael!" her right arm stretched toward him, the palm of her hand up and open.

He made her wait another few seconds, so paralyzed was he with fear, and then after taking a deep breath he rose and walked slowly up the aisle, his eyes glued to his shoes. He handed her the note, and she looked at it for a couple of seconds.

"Tomorrow morning, Michael, have your parents bring you to school. I need to see them in my office."

"You mean, my father?" Trembling, he found it hard to talk.

Her face turned red. "Yes, I mean your father. Fifteen minutes early." Though she had been told his mother was deceased, he was one of the boys who never gave her any trouble, and so she had forgotten.

The next morning at 7:45 a.m. his father went to Helen Mulroy's office while he waited in the hall. All of the O'Keefe teachers were female, and most unmarried.

"It's a pleasure to finally meet you," he said, holding his gray fedora by the brim. "I'm sorry to be here under *these* circumstances."

His father was not handsome, and he had a prominent bump on his nose, a childhood fracture from his stickball days. But he was nice enough looking with his soft blue eyes and good teeth, well dressed and well mannered; the kind of man who struck women as a gentleman.

"Would you like to see the note?" she asked.

"Michael told me it has every dirty word in his vocabulary."

"It sounds like we are talking about the same note."

"Then I don't need to see it. I need to apologize on behalf of our family, and can only hope this doesn't reflect his entire history with you."

"Oh, Mr. Stein, there's no need for an apology. There isn't anything in that note I haven't seen or heard before. And as for Michael's history, as you put it, he is one of the most wonderful boys I have ever had in my class. And I've been teaching here almost 15 years."

Sam's eyes moistened with emotion. He was handling this with aplomb, but he had felt disgraced.

"He will receive a lecture from me. You can be sure of that. Your kindness and understanding will not be wasted."

Helen Mulroy's heart fluttered with hope. This was a man she could spend an evening with. She stood. "I just want you to know. I am tearing this note up now." She did that and threw the pieces in the wastebasket. "I have the feeling he's learned a lesson for life."

"I have that feeling too," Sam replied. "Again, thank you for your understanding."

She extended her arm. He shook her hand and turned to go.

"Mr. Stein. I want you to know that I'm making Michael a movie boy."

He had visions of Hollywood—Mickey Rooney and the other child stars. But for only a second. The movie boys, he knew from Michael, set up the projector in the various classrooms when needed for science films. These were boys deemed trustworthy, who wouldn't horse around and ruin the equipment. It was a vote of confidence, but not Hollywood.

"He'll be pleased," Sam said, wondering if this might encourage a raft of dirty letters. But what did he know? He wasn't a teacher.

———

O'Keefe occupied the whole block, though more than half of it was playground. The boys played "ledge-ball," bouncing a rubber ball off the concrete ledge running round the building. The girls jumped rope and played hopscotch. There was a *shelter house* in the playground, about the size of a two-car garage, where they stored sports equipment, bats and balls and other basics that were obtainable so long as some security (like keys) was posted. The chalked sidewalks and ricocheting balls produced its share of merriment unless one of the scarier bullies showed up. And in one unfortunate turnabout, one of those bullies was attacked by an avenging mob of smaller kids.

"They kept pounding him!" Michael told Hazel when he got home. "From behind and the front and the side. It must have been twelve on one. And when I saw blood, I wanted to call the police or a teacher or someone! But then they stopped, he was bleeding so badly."

In reality, it was a cut nose and lip, but this lurid tale had resonated with Hazel. And even after he had finished telling it, she was still turning her head from side to side in sympathy.

"They gonna give him cancer with all that pounding. I wonder where his *mama* is, that he gets into that kind of trouble."

Though that wasn't really trouble in her lexicon. Earlier that year, when she and her cousins had gone to a funeral in Louisiana (a rare excursion for her), they had to drive straight through, almost twenty-four hours without stopping for anything but gas, because to stop was to be harassed, possibly lynched. And while the bloody nose and lip this bully suffered was trifling in comparison, it evoked the more grotesque dangers she faced not only in the deep south, but a bus ride away on the west side.

———————

After Sam fired Hazel, she rented a room from her cousin. For the next several years, she worked as a pastry chef at a Loop restaurant, which entailed late hours and a long walk from the bus stop to her cousin's after dark. One winter evening, carrying (as usual) a large canvas bag, she felt a dull, throbbing, pain in her upper back and left arm as she trudged down the sidewalk in the frigid night air. She paused to catch her breath. It was then that she may have felt a tug on the straps of the bag she held so tightly, this from a man wearing a wool knit cap over his head and ears, his face unshaven, with shadows under his eyes darker than the dark brown of his skin.

"Don't pay me no neveh mind, boy," she might have warned him.

And then this man might've knocked her down, which wouldn't have taken much. Though we don't know that happened. We only know from the autopsy that she had a coronary. Two of the bags' straps had been ripped, the remaining two still wrapped around her wrist. It didn't appear that anything had been taken, the bag still full to the brim: a bulky wool sweater, scarf, beret, earmuffs, a hardbound copy of the bible, an unused bus transfer, and some loose change at the bottom totaling the exact amount of carfare, the kind of bag that Sam was so certain was filled with food from their kitchen.

If a friend of Michael's hadn't sent him the Sun-Times article about this and other incidents on the west side of the city, he would never have known what happened. Her anonymity would have continued, like a hitless streak of one of her beloved White Sox players. Because in all those years that she took him from boyhood to manhood, neither the phone nor the doorbell ever rang for her. Nor did she blow out a birthday candle or receive a present, or were

her own needs, tastes or wishes in any other way consid-
ered relevant. And now this brutal end, he would stew, the
awful ambiguity of it, all alone, without anyone to look out
for her the way she had looked out for him.

5

AFTER RUTH HARRIS died, Michael's Aunt Florence, his father's older sister, stepped into the breach. She had had a rough childhood of her own with her drunken mother, Hannah. After high school, she left the country for Buenos Aires where she trained with a dance troupe, and then Paris where she met her husband-to-be, Sergei, a Count from czarist Russia who had fled a less formidable foe than Hannah—the Bolsheviks. For months the hotel that Sergei's family had frequented accepted his I.O.U.'s in the belief they would be rewarded, as they had been in the past, when the rebellion fizzled. But that didn't happen this time, and when they finally asked him to leave he needed money for an apartment and so he pawned the gems he had smuggled out of Russia. And after he and Florence had run through that money, he tendered his ring and watch for pawn as well.

"I won't take them," the pawnbroker said.

"And why is that?" Sergei exclaimed. "It's a star sapphire, a beautiful one, and the watch is a Patek Philippe.

They're worth more than the gems."

"I don't want you to lose them. I could use some help around here, and you know good jewelry as well as I do."

So Sergei went to work for the pawnbroker.

"This was lucky," he crowed to Florence six months later. "Between your salary and mine, we're covering our expenses."

"Depends on how you define expenses." She was the skeptic when it came to the pawnbroker. "Your boss isn't as noble as you think. He sold the gems you pawned for a small fortune."

And that was all Florence had to say, that they hadn't been saved, but rather taken advantage of, working, as Sergei did, twelve hours a days and six days a week's while she held two jobs (dancing at night), all to make ends meet.

"We can live in the states," he said, uttering the words she had been waiting to hear. She had received letters from her father and brothers that their plumbing supplies business was doing great. Indeed the whole U.S. economy was on fire, the "roaring '20's" they called it.

"Who knows?" he added, "that may have been my destiny...to live in the U.S. How else can you explain why my English tutor had an American accent?"

She smiled.

"Just get me a visa," he added, "or they won't let me in."

When Florence and Sergei arrived in the U.S., the '20's had no roar for them. He found employment as a watch repairman at Marshall Field & Co. where he earned less than he had at the pawnbroker's. She earned an even more modest amount as a sales clerk in Field's antique jewelry department. After twenty years in the U.S. of trying to save money to open their own jewelry store, it still seemed a faraway goal.

"I'll talk to Sam," she told Sergei. "Maybe he can help. We'll give him stock."

Sam found this amusing, the idea of stock in a jewelry store. He knew his sister wasn't a businessperson, but he wanted to be supportive. "I'll give you $2,000," he said. "We'll call it a loan, but don't lose any sleep over repaying me."

That was enough for Florence and Sergei to buy the inventory they couldn't get on consignment. They opened their store, and by their fourth year in business Michael would visit them in the late afternoons. He was only two blocks away at the synagogue where he attended Hebrew School. He enjoyed the homey feel of the store, especially its quainter items like the pocket watches Sergei had bought at Parisian flea markets, though the real ambiance was supplied by Sergei himself, his Czar Nicholas mustache and aristocratically long fingernails, his silver cigarette holder, and techy jeweler's loupe mounted to his tortoise shell spectacles.

"This is nothing!" he would reassure the customer, opening the watchcase right there on the spot and blowing a hair out that had lassoed the mainspring.

"For God's sake, just take the watch in and give them a claim ticket!" Florence would scold him afterward. "And then we can charge something."

But it wasn't in him, these tricks of the trade. And if the customer took for granted such honesty and transparency, and wasn't the least bit grateful, that too was lost on Sergei whose own integrity was his guide. And though Florence scolded him, she wasn't much better and in a hundred other ways was too genteel to play the game.

When her mother, in one of her more insane states of inebriation, tossed a brick through their store window, they closed up and never reopened. By the time Michael dropped by days later, the plate glass window had been replaced, but obscuring the new one was a huge FOR RENT sign in bright red letters. His aunt and uncle would take on family obligations in exchange for a stipend from the plumbing supplies company. Though he loved being with his aunt and uncle, as time went on he knew he didn't want to *be* them. They had no financial security or independence. They were on Sam's dole, as far as he could tell, only a pawn away from the ring or the watch.

6

MICHAEL HAD NEVER seen an apartment like the Hartfield's. It wasn't just the size and location, though a 12,000 square foot penthouse overlooking Central Park was impressive. It was the elegance of the building and the apartment and its furnishings and artwork, all set in the excitement and vitality of Manhattan. He felt good about having decided to stay with Hal for Thanksgiving. Far better than a frenzied back and forth to Chicago only three weeks before the Christmas break.

"Wash up for dinner, kids!"

Hal's mother found new and different ways to annoy her son.

"Yes Mumsy," he responded mockingly.

Margaret Hartfield stood at a large mirror near the front door adjusting a brooch her husband, Mortimer, had brought her from Scotland. She wasn't above accepting bribes to tolerate his dalliances. She freshened her lipstick, turning her head from side to side, clamping a tissue between her lips to blot the final coat. And then, as always, pleased with her reflection, she joined them in the dining room where she pressed a buzzer and, within seconds, a light skinned African-American man emerged from the kitchen in a white jacket with tails.

Until that moment, Michael had imagined his family the social equal of Hal's. Forget that the Harrisons were one of the wealthiest and best-known families in America. Michael had learned from his father how to level the playing field and so, as he saw it, their parity began with their two Ivy Leaguers. And though the Harrison railroad empire was a part of American history, Sergei's family in czarist Russia was one for the books as well, his father a builder of the Trans-Siberian railway and his uncle, Count Witte, the most respected of the czarist Prime Ministers.

"Comin Miss Hartfield," the butler's voice a velvety bass. "I was just uncorkin the champagne." Walking briskly toward the dining room, he carried an open bottle with a small white hand towel wrapped around the neck.

"This is Roscoe," Hal said, introducing him to Michael.

"How *do* you do, Sir," said Roscoe, who stopped and bowed his head slightly.

"I'm fine," Michael replied, and all he could think of at that moment was Hal's joke about the valet ... or maybe it wasn't a joke.

They took their seats. The place settings were elegant. Plates from Italy, silver from England, and crystal wine and water glasses from preceding Harrison generations. As for the menu, this was not your grandma's turkey, sweet potatoes and cranberries. Rather a culinary masterpiece of the Hartfield's cook who, in his prime, had been the chef of a top Manhattan restaurant.

"Wittgenstein is a charlatan!" bellowed Mortimer, raising his wine glass ceremoniously, signaling the debate he sought with his son and friend, the surrogates tonight of his old pal and Harvard classmate, Stuart Brin. They were spirited rivals, Hartfield and Brin, the latter taking Cornell's department more in the direction of Wittgenstein and the Linguistics, with Hartfield and hence Columbia in the sway of the more traditional Greek and British philosophers.

"Dad, Cornell's not the only school teaching the Linguistics," Hal said. "Last time I saw your Columbia program, you had a course on them as well."

"That's true. I was outvoted. If I had my druthers, that wouldn't have occurred. He's bogus and tiresome and…"

Hartfield closed his eyes and clutched the bridge of his nose with his thumb and forefinger, mocking the histrionics of Wittgenstein that had so beguiled his disciples and amused his detractors.

As the debate continued, Hal grew agitated, clearing his throat and patting his shirt pocket to make sure his cigarettes were there. Margaret circulated the platters and scolded Mortimer for not eating and not including Hal's "guest" in the conversation, but otherwise stayed out of it.

It wasn't until dessert and brandy that Mortimer dialed it down, reminiscing about his own college days when he and Brin were at Harvard, and Frederick Horton was there in the history department.

"Hal and I may have been the only father and son to have both taken Horton's class," Mortimer said. "Keep in mind, it's not just the gap in years that would have to match up but it's Horton's move from Harvard to Cornell."

Hartfield was the same age as his wife but, as against her genuinely red hair (no gray) and her commitment to cosmetics, his bushy eyebrows and thick, gray hair made him look older.

"He was a young pup in his Harvard days. Had just come back from Oxford and was a teaching asslistant," Hartfield continued.

"It's hard to imagine Professor Horton as a T.A.," Michael said to Mortimer, "the way he lectures."

"He's a bit of a windbag now, is he?" Mortimer responded, recalling that tendency of Horton's even as a T.A.

"I'm afraid he is." Michael glanced at Hal who had known since his prep school days that Freddie's Class at Cornell was a joke.

They concluded their dinner discussion with more general topics—Democrats versus Republicans, America versus Europe—and then he and Hal were off for a walk, puffing on dark, thick Cuban cigars Hal had lifted from his father's humidor.

"You saw his good side," Hal said, in need of a reality check.

"Your father is an accomplished man, with a zest for disputation, and cool friends like Brin."

"Or he can be just plain boring. And pretentious; you can count on that. I mean, '*Dr.* Hartfield!' Give me a break. When I was 10 or 12, he'd do the doctor thing to get a seat on the aisle or a choice parking spot at the stadium. When I got older, though, I realized he was actually serious about it, about wanting to be called 'doctor.'"

"What's your problem with that, that he's not a *medical* doctor?"

"Yah!" Hal said, singing the word, his sarcasm oozing. "Isn't there a moral issue if someone gets special privileges available for medical emergencies, when his real function is to explain Hegel or Kant?"

By the time they had returned to the apartment, it seemed Hal was just warming up as a critic of his father. They went upstairs and, true to form, he fell asleep the moment his head hit the pillow while Michael lay awake processing it all. There was the butler and the cook, Margaret's pretenses and Mortimer's intensity; and last but not least, the father-son rivalry. It was Hal's words, "when I got older" that stuck in Michael's head before he too slipped into sleep. It reminded him of the Mark Twain adage, that by the time you're thirty your father will have improved considerably. And if that were the case, Hal and his father had more than ten years to wait.

7

MICHAEL'S GRANDFATHER, JOSEPH Stein, immigrated to America with his parents when he was sixteen. They settled in Chicago where he apprenticed with a plumber. And three years later, his parents' decided it was time for him to marry.

"Marry?" he asked incredulously.

"You'll be twenty next month," his father said, "with a thick accent.

"How old were you?" Joseph asked.

"Eighteen. You're an old man. And Yosef, do I have a girl for you!" Whereupon, magically, Joseph's mother appeared.

"She's a beauty!" she added, her accent like her husband's.

"She would know," his father piled on. "She's like your mother."

Now this was problematical, it would seem from Joseph's expression. He loved his mother, but he wasn't looking for another.

"She's not like me at all," his mother said, more perceptively. "This girl's the dickens, I tell you. They're all raving about her. So high-spirited! A stick of dynamite."

"What does she look like?" Joseph asked. This was sounding better.

"I'll show you a picture."

Joseph was touched, because he had given this subject no thought, and that wasn't smart. He was going to be twenty.

"Who is it?" he asked.

His mother didn't answer. She was rummaging through dresser drawers, trying to find the photo.

"Here it is!" she shouted with relief, holding an envelope covered with Polish stamps. She pulled the photo out of the envelope.

"What do you think?" she asked, holding it up to the light.

He didn't know what to say, this all seemed so random. They still hadn't mentioned her name. And the photo was fuzzy, though he had to admit she looked cute...and frisky.

"Who is it?" he asked again.

"It's Esther's youngest daughter, Hannah. She's your cousin. It's okay, though, I asked the rabbi. It's a *second* cousin. He said there would be no Jews in this country if they couldn't marry cousins. He didn't mean it, of course, but you get the point."

He didn't say anything.

"If it's okay with you, I'm going to ask her to come and stay with us for awhile."

And again he didn't say anything. He just wondered how long he'd have to wait.

————————

They married four months later, before she was visibly pregnant. Joseph's mother had gotten what she bargained for—the stick of dynamite. Hannah's two older brothers, who had escorted her to the states, would remain in Chicago as well, though not with their sister in the Stein apartment. They had their own place. It smelled like a brewery, and Hannah hung around there enough to pick up the habit. The only prolonged periods she stayed sober were during her three pregnancies, the first Florence, and then Sam followed by Max.

The fact that his wife was an alcoholic and he had no normal life at home, kept Joseph at the office from dawn to dusk. Sam could recall the evening his father came home even later than usual, with his momentous announcement. Sam was 14 at the time. He was near their front door with Florence and Max when his father arrived and, with his hat still on, exclaimed to the three of them, "I've got important news, *mein kinder*! We're going to have our own company, *Stein & Sons*!"

They knew nothing about such ambitions, that their father, a salesman for a plumbing supplies contractor, could go into business for himself. For Florence, the oldest who had just turned 18, this news was jarring. If it offered a future for the boys, that wasn't likely to include her, there being no place for a girl in business, not in those days or in their family. And so it was then and there that she decided to leave the country for South America and Europe.

As for the plumbing supplies business, it did well from the start, though it was hard to know how much credit was due Joseph. You could do no wrong in the business world in the mid-1920's, King Midas, so it seemed, touching everything in sight. It wouldn't be until four years later that the bubble would burst and, when it did, Sam was in a bubble of his own—academia. The economic cataclysm was the biggest news story in the world, but Sam's workload at school hadn't diminished. Nor had the erudition of his professors who now, for added spice, sprinkled in sage observations related to these events. What finally drove reality home was that his family couldn't pay his tuition any longer. Joseph needed every penny he had to keep the business alive. It was Ruth who got through to Sam with the message.

"Dearest Sam," she wrote (though she was barely a mile away at the Library and could have said all this in person), "I know how much you love your studies and the university, and how deeply disappointing this is, that you won't have the money for school, but really, if you did, it's not a time for contemplation. It's a time for action. It's a war out there, my Darling, a battle for survival, and your filial duty requires you don the your armor and pull your family through."

Less than a week into his third year, Sam dropped out of the University of Chicago to run the family business. Six months later, Joseph died, the stresses of the Depression more attributable to his demise than the reason given in his death certificate. As for Sam's academic aspirations, nostalgia would take it from there. His friends in later years, certainly his poker buddies who had never graduated high school, weren't aware he hadn't finished college, so erudite did he seem to them and so chauvinistic was he about the U of C.

Would that his family was similarly impressed! They weren't, and they weren't likely to confuse his BS with any bachelor of science the colleges were conferring. Elaine and Michael, whose educations would include elite graduate degrees, became practiced at humoring him. And Florence, well read and self-taught, was loath to contradict for fear of jeopardizing her stipend. As for Sergei, whose education and upbringing had been so privileged he lacked the grit to make a living, he was bemused by the bombast, hanging around Sam's liquor cabinet for some cognac to wash the vodka down, and that would be around the time Roscoe was clearing away the brandy snifters at the Hartfields.

8

"SO LET ME look at you!" Sam said to him, eyes glistening with pride. They were at Midway Airport. Michael's father and Elaine had been waiting for him at the baggage claim area.

"A real Ivy Leaguer!"

Michael glanced around to make sure there was no one he knew.

"You've grown," Elaine said, trying to keep it factual.

"Let me take that!" Sam grabbed his duffel. It was loaded with books and much heavier than he had expected. "What do you have in here? A body?"

He wanted his bag back, but his father was still stronger and on the move already. At Sam's pace they were at the parking area in no time, the white Caddie looking large and gaudy as compared to the VW's and the other imports on the Cornell campus.

"So tell us about Thanksgiving!" his father said, once they were in the car and on their way. He had that special lilt in his voice to signal the importance of this occasion. "You're keeping company with royalty when you're talking about the Harrisons. Henry tells me the old man, Rupert, is coming close to a decision to run for Governor."

"It's not the Harrisons I was with, Dad. It's the Hartfields. And Hal's Grandfather is in a coma. He's been that way for a month."

Elaine squirmed in the front seat.

"It's the best kept secret in New York," Michael added. "I guess the press still has some respect for family privacy."

Much of Sam's info came from his Monday night poker game, buddies like Henry Greenberg. Henry's news wasn't always the freshest, but it didn't usually stink this badly. Hal's grandfather, Rupert Harrison, who in past years had been mentioned as a New York gubernatorial candidate, had suffered a massive stroke.

"Is that true?" Sam asked.

Elaine craned her head around to the back seat, determined to change the subject. "How's the philosophy major? And how did you decide that? I mean, you've just begun."

"It's the only class where I don't look at my watch. I figured that's got to mean something."

She studied the contours of his duffel bag, books pushing the canvas out in every direction.

"My God!" she exclaimed. "That's a lot of books, and I thought Lit was bad." Elaine was doing graduate work in Literature at the U of I's Circle Campus.

"You have a lot of books in Philosophy, but you only read parts of them."

"That would be nice," she said, "parts..."

"In philosophy, it's not what you know. It's what you don't know. You learn to think."

As he said this, he could imagine the smirk on his father's face. Selling bathroom fixtures took salesmanship, not thinking. Paying his son's tuition took money, not thinking. When he had to drop out of college, it wasn't for a lack of thinking. What his son didn't know could fill the books in that duffel of his...but his father didn't say any of this. He didn't want to spoil this holiday break they'd all been waiting for.

They were heading east now along the broad expanse of the Midway where he could see the white stone buildings of the University of Chicago, structures his father revered so irrationally that Cornell must have looked dinky to him, like they could have used a little Rockefeller money in Ithaca to replace those cement block dorms.

———————

Though there were no photos of Michael's mother that survived the warehouse fire, there were some supplied later by family and friends. Occasionally his sister would ask him to go through those with her, most recently the week before he left for Cornell.

"Do you not remember this?" she had asked, showing him a photo he had seen many times.

Taken on the Midway by his Uncle Sergei, it was a grainy black and white of him, Elaine and their parents seated on a park bench across from the hospital. The day was bright and his mother, who had a large headscarf on which made her face look smaller, was squinting badly from a sun much brighter than the lighting of her room.

At their ages then, he and Elaine weren't allowed in the oncology ward and thus his mother had been wheeled to this park bench. You could see a bit of her hospital gown underneath her coat, and part of the wheelchair at the outer edge of the picture. Elaine's long legs previewed her imminent growth spurt. And there he was, the pipsqueak next to his mother, squinting as badly as she.

"I don't remember it, no," He was six, almost seven when his mother died, and you would think at that age he'd have a memory of her. But he didn't.

Which was difficult for Elaine to accept. At the time of her mother's death, Elaine was 10, and those incremental years made all the difference. She had girlfriends and their mothers who were determined to keep the memory of Ruth Stein alive, in fact held an annual charity drive in her name that Elaine would, in later years, help organize. That was very different from the Sam Stein cocoon, sealed off at home and in the workplace. And so, by adulthood, Michael looked to Elaine as the expert on their mother—what she might have liked, disliked, approved or disapproved, her values, and her ways.

"Now here's one where she was looking good," Elaine said, showing him another photo, his mother holding him at the edge of a wading pool, about four years before she died.

And indeed that was a photo he could take some pleasure in, because his mother looked beautiful and healthy and happy holding him, a scene he had absorbed so thoroughly over the years he thought he remembered it. Though that couldn't have been possible at age 2. Or was it?

———————

A scene Michael could never have witnessed (because kids weren't permitted in the oncology ward) took place in his mother's hospital room—she and his father dancing. When it was clear she was doomed, they wanted one last tango. They couldn't unhook the monitoring equipment and so the dance steps, made difficult, as they were, by his mother's condition, were further impeded by dangling cords. With it all, however, they were impressive, an authentic Argentinian tango that Florence had taught Sam after her early travels abroad. Too bad no one was around with a camera, but those who heard from complaining nurses, and might have seen them tango in happier times, had an image of it more lifelike than a photo.

———————

The Caddie was big, but not big enough for a Sam Stein explosion, imminent, Michael sensed, from the silence and nervous cough. It was no picnic living with the man, he reflected, and yet this was Elaine's plight year-round. The new apartment where they were headed was large, he had heard, compared to the flat they had in South Shore. But while that was true and Elaine had her own bedroom and bath, it wasn't a matter of physical space. Their father had grown even more controlling, his relationship with his girlfriend, Maude, an irritant. He was quick to the boiling point, so unpleasant that Elaine would have had her own apartment if she weren't an impoverished student again.

"You're too big for your britches!" the volcano erupted, Sam craning around to glare at Michael.

"Dad!" Elaine pleaded, which meant don't spoil things, though Sam was at the point of no return.

"A couple of days on Park Avenue and your father's a fool! Is that it? This is the payback I get on my tuition money—a snob? You better look in the mirror, Michael. Your beard's still patchy. You've got a long way to go before you know the answers. If I thought Rupert Harrison was going to run for Governor, that's not such a crazy thought. I don't care if he's dead and buried. The man was mentioned for that office before you were born. So don't think you know it all!"

"Sorry Dad. I don't think I know it all."

"Then why do you say things like that?" his father exclaimed, his voice still rising. "Because you're a smart aleck? Am I supposed to know he's in a coma? Tell me, am I?"

"No, of course not. I'm sorry."

"Then don't let it happen again, you hear me."

"Yes. It won't happen again."

They pulled up to a stone tower building, distinctive looking with its handsome frescoes between each floor. A world apart from their second floor apartment in the brick six-flat, this was high up on the 20th with a clear view of the lake.

"My coat's back there," Sam said, calm now and pointing to the hook next to where Michael had been sitting.

He handed the jacket to his father as Elaine opened the front passenger door and stepped out.

"Go ahead without me," their father said. "I've got to tell them to give me a wash."

As they walked through the lobby, Michael gaped a bit

at the swanky appointments, the lighting and the reception desk an elegant marble. There would be no mistaking this for the tiny lobby of their old six-flat with its dingy lighting and scratched up mail boxes. He put his arm around Elaine, bonding, as they always did, over their father's temper. To look at their faces, the sibling relationship was obvious, actually striking.

"The old stack still blows," he said, smiling.

"I ought to get him a T-shirt that says 'This skin is thin.'" she responded. "You handled that well."

"With him, the apology works like magic. How's your love life?" he asked, changing the subject.

Her smile changed to a frown.

"Don't ask," she replied.

And he wouldn't, he knew. Wouldn't ever ask again.

"Come to Chicago! It'll be fun!" Michael shouted over the crackling of the long-distance phone connection.

It was a call from Hal. His return to Manhattan for Christmas had been a fiasco. His father was in Scotland for a conference, and his mother at the Harrison's winter home in Palm Beach. The apartment was empty.

"I'll be there, man! Tomorrow, if I can get something." That was the last thing Hal said before he showed up in Chicago at their building at 10:00 a.m. the next morning.

"A Mr. Hartfield downstairs," the receptionist in the lobby announced over the intercom. And a minute later Michael opened their front door to his grinning roommate.

"6:30 out of LaGuardia!" Hal trumpeted.

They shook hands exuberantly and Michael didn't let go as he pulled Hal in. His father and Elaine were standing there. She was in her bathrobe."

"Good to meet you, Sir," Hal said to Sam. "I've heard a lot about you."

His father shook Hal's hand, impressed as always with young men who said "Sir" and had the personality, in Sam's words, to light a fire right from the start. That's how Sam chose his salesmen, and that's how, he believed, you get somewhere.

"We're delighted you could join us," Elaine said, pushing her hair back hurriedly. She too had decided, for reasons quite different from her father's, that she liked what she saw—indeed was instantly taken with Hal. Which was surprising because he was much younger than her and had that privileged collegiate look she had gotten away from at Circle.

As for Michael, this visit was a joy. He and his Lab School friends played indoor tennis with Hal at the Field House, and pool and billiards at the Reynolds Club. In the evening, they went to flicks, as Hal called them, artsy films Elaine would select and, as their graduate school guru, critique with impressive insight. Her presence, Hal could not help but reflect, was a bonus, the attention he got from her in contrast to his distracted parents. He didn't mind her nagging him about his smoking; to the contrary, was touched by her concern, which is more than he could say about his mother who was herself a smoker, and his father whose thoughts centered around his work and himself.

"And now for the finale!" Michael exclaimed. "I can't have you saying you were in Chicago and didn't go to The

Cellar."

This was tongue in cheek because The Cellar was hardly a tourist attraction. But he did think it was a hip place and for this final night of Hal's in Chicago, there was a poetry reading by one of the country's most respected young poets, Stefan Hirsch. And Hal, he knew, loved poetry.

"What's The Cellar?" Hal asked.

"Just trust me, man.

"Okay. Tell me when, and I'm game."

They left after dinner on a mile-long walk that seemed shorter than that to Hal, he was so stimulated by the sights and sounds of Hyde Park. It reminded him, he said, of the Village.

A coffee shop and bookstore, The Cellar accommodated about 50 people. They had a full house with the Hirsch reading, but there were a couple of standing room tickets still available. Michael grabbed them, finding some space for Hal and him along the back wall.

"Well, what do you know!" he muttered after checking the place out.

At the opposite end of the room, there was a girl who stood and looked their way. She couldn't see them, he knew, so nearsighted was she without her glasses. And taking advantage of this infirmity, he stared with abandon, remembering that curvy body within the shapeless smock she wore. It got him excited, actually, and while Hirsch must have read a couple of dozen poems that evening, he wouldn't remember a word.

He and Roberta were seldom apart the summer between his junior and senior year in high school, though on this particular evening at the Cellar in a crowd of no more than fifty, he'd succeed in losing track of her. By the time he and Hal had followed everyone out the door, she was nowhere to be found and he was furious.

"What the hell!"

"The hell what, man?" Hal asked.

"Damn side doors!" He hadn't noticed the emergency exits at the sides of the room that had been opened.

And as for Hal, he was oblivious to everything but the poetry.

"I liked that poem about love and science," Hal said.

They were in two different worlds, Hal thinking of poetry, and he, of Roberta.

Couldn't she have put her glasses on, he stewed? Was she still that self-conscious? Maybe she *had* seen him, and had *chosen* to duck out through a side door. Maybe she was seeing someone else. Whatever! It had been a couple of years He'd have to call her to get the answers. And, then again, even if he didn't get the answers, he'd have to call her.

———

The Fields owned their home, a small house on a quiet street lined with a thick row of elms that provided much needed shade in that hot summer he and Roberta dated and he hung out there.

"I'm here!" Hyman Field would announce each weekday shortly after 5:00 p.m., having returned from his brokerage office a few minutes away. He would shower and change, then sweep the sidewalk and mow the lawn or read the newspaper while his wife, Sarah, prepared dinner. Rober-

ta's mother was always home, it seemed, and how they got food into the place was a mystery since he couldn't recall a grocery run. And yet there was lots of it, food, that is, and he could attest to how good it was, since he had dinner with them most evenings.

"We're going, Mom," Roberta announced after the two of them had cleared the table and put the dirty silverware and dishes in the sink.

"Go! You're in the way. You have a good time," she'd say joyfully, her sink runneth over.

And they'd leave in Elaine's Chevy (on loan to him that summer while she was away), bound for their usual destination, the drive-in theater where they went gratis on his father's pass, the card dog-eared from its repeated use. A real windfall, this car and the pass, because the back seat of Elaine's car was as big and comfy as the Field's living room couch and far more private.

If you're wondering how they could have watched the same movie again and again, it having no merit cinematically, only teenagers with their hormones raging could have answered that. Suffice it to say that had this been live theatre and one of the actors taken ill, they could have gone on as stand-ins, so familiar were they with the dialogue. And though her parents never asked where they were going, a drive-in theater would not have occurred to them. That was invented for these young lovers and this coming of age, their rite of spring...or in this case, summer.

9

TO BE OR not to be wasn't the question the freshmen boys at Cornell asked when it came to fraternities; few Hamlets among them, the vast majority joined.

"You know," Michael said to Hal, "fraternity rush begins next week."

It had been there, on the calendar, all this time, the inaugural rush date in the second week of the second semester, though until now, it seemed to Michael frustratingly distant. Sure, he had his friendship with Hal, but the campus social life revolved around fraternities and sororities—the parties, the booze, and the Gatsby style living quarters (the frat he coveted, at the edge of a cliff with its own waterfall). That, and not these red brick dorms, felt like college.

But not to Hal.

"I hate it! Reminds me of Grovener," he would say, "though even Grovener didn't divide the boys into Jew and gentile." (At Cornell, in those days, the Jewish boys pledged "Jewish houses" and the gentile boys pledged "gentile houses").

"That's because they didn't have any Jews," Michael responded, laboring to defend this bifurcation that, with his U-High background, was no less foreign to him.

"You should rush some gentile houses," Hal said, his thought being that the two of them could rush together. Some guys who were good friends did that, went through as a package.

"No, I couldn't be one of two or three Jews found gentile enough to be with the gentiles, when they've black-balled every other Jew."

"Well, aren't the Jewish houses excluding the gentiles and even some of the Jews they consider too Jewish?" Hal asked, both truth and logic on his side.

This was their sorest subject, one that Hal, in particular, was exercised about. Cornell, in his view, wasn't some throwback prep school. It was one of the great universities of the world and, to his way of thinking, this Greek system was an anomaly.

"Look," he said, in an effort to find common ground. "I signed up for rushing. Does that show some open-mindedness?"

"Yes, but if you don't actually go with a house, what will you do?"

"Are you saying there's no life on this campus without a fraternity?"

Now that was a question Michael didn't have a good answer for because it did seem a matter of life and death to him, even as to *which* frat, especially the one with the waterfall.

"Well, I'm sure," he conceded, "there are going to be guys not going fraternity. You'll need to pair up with someone, though, if you don't want to be in a single."

Hal blanched. The dreaded word, *single*. His life at Grovener had been made even worse, as he viewed it, because he had always been in a single.

"You mean, I have to start looking around?" Hal asked. "You've definitely made up your mind?"

Michael took a deep breath. This was a trail, he had thought, that had a fork in it. For now, he'd go one way and Hal the other. But these paths would merge again. It wasn't forever. They'd still be living together in the dorm for the rest of this year. And if sophomore year he lived in the fraternity house, still he'd be in an apartment his last two years, and he and Hal could be together again.

"Well, not definitely," he replied, "but I'm going to rush and try my luck…and if I get in…."

"In the house you want?" Hal said.

"Yes. There's one in particular I'm interested in. And their pledge program is virtually nonexistent."

Hal held his tongue. Now this was a game changer! Because even more anachronistic than the religious divide, in his view, was hazing.

"Do they have any non-Jewish members?" Hal asked

"Yes. I happen to know there's one. Do you want me to ask?"

"Sure, ask," Hal said, feeling the weight of his own hypocrisy.

———

"I asked someone I know," Michael reported to Hal the

next day. "It's not like it's an official policy, but the fact is that everyone's Jewish except one guy, and it happens I know him very well; he was a year ahead of me at the Lab School. He's considered a special case, because he's Negro. That's pretty laudable, don't you think?"

"Michael, I mean, Yippee! They took the Negro. Do you want my real opinion? That's the least they could do to demonstrate a sense of humanity. We're on different wavelengths, my friend, if you consider it laudable, because I consider it patronizing."

"It really isn't. He's a good friend who I know extremely well. I'm sure they liked him and didn't care about the color of his skin. And as for it being patronizing, I don't know what that means. I only know that if a Jewish fraternity doesn't understand discrimination, that doesn't say much for them. And if they felt it was the kind of thing a Jewish house should do, like I said, I think that's laudable, and that's why I like this house."

"Well, maybe they'll like you," Hal said, with some bitterness. "And maybe one day you'll explain to me why he's not being discriminated against but I am, and why that's okay."

"You've got choices! That's why. More than I do. But *he* didn't. This isn't Howard University. And that's the difference."

Which was how it went that week and the next, Michael pointing out to Hal the good, even admirable things about the frat he wanted, and Hal hating the whole thing but professing to have an open mind. As the rushing phase came to a close with bids out and the boys making their decisions (Michael couldn't conceal his joy at getting the house by the waterfall), Hal caved and accepted the bid of a blueblood, hard-drinking gentile fraternity impressed by his preppy looks and Harrison pedigree.

"It was a big mistake!" Hal would complain to him only a couple of days later, chaffing under the lash of his pledge master. "He kept us there for hours, saying the same thing over and over again. When I couldn't keep my mouth shut any longer, I asked him 'Gene, why the repetition? What's that supposed to accomplish?' And he looked at me like I was crazy. I thought he was deadpanning.

"'Don't call me Gene,' he said. Unless and until you become a member, I'm the Exalted Pledgemaster. When you see me on campus, you say 'good morning, Exalted Pledgemaster,' and I want to see a big shit-eater on your face. And if it's afternoon, you say 'good afternoon, Exalted Pledgemaster.' And don't get that wrong. I don't want to hear 'good morning' in the afternoon or 'good afternoon' in the morning. And if you're standing there with a friend, I better get the same respect you'd show me if you were standing alone. I don't care if you're standing there with ten friends. You got it? You could be talking to your professor, and I get the respect and I get the eater as well. You see me. I get it!

"'Now let's get back to what you think is repetition. It may sound like that to you, but it isn't. I'm perfect and therefore incapable of repetition. You understand that? Those concepts are mutually exclusive—me and repetition, me and imperfection. You only think you're hearing the same thing over and over. But, as I educate you, you will understand that you're not, that there are different shades of meaning in every sentence and every word that comes out of my mouth. I'm like the leaves of a tree—infinitely variegated. Like nature, perfect!'

"'So don't let me hear anything from you that I can mistake for criticism. Just *bask* in my perfection. Because those who don't will clean Triphammer Bridge with a toothbrush and then clean their mouths out with that same brush. It won't be pretty, my Plebes. It won't be pretty.'"

10

"WHO YOU STUDYING with these days?" a question Michael asked Hal, who didn't know how to answer because he thought the truth appalling. And, on the other hand, if he lied there would be more questions. So he changed the subject.

"Let me figure *this* out," he responded, looking down at his boots; one was ripped at the top. "I snagged this on something. Don't know what." He took it off, looked inside, and made a couple of observations that made it even more clear this was a dodge.

"Just get new ones!" Michael responded irritably. "Or wear them the way they are. That's fashionable, the worn-in natty look."

"You're telling me about fashion, man?" Hal glared at him disapprovingly. "We get a lot of rain in this place, in case you haven't noticed. And these aren't waterproof anymore."

This had been the quality of their dialogue—irritating and evasive. Since pledging had begun, they didn't study together anymore, and had none of the old talks they used to have before falling asleep. That wasn't possible because Hal didn't get to bed at a decent hour. This conversation they were now having was the exception, a freezing rain in February that had driven everyone back to their rooms for shelter or rain gear.

"That guy still a maniac?" he asked Hal, certain the lousy mood wasn't due to the weather.

"One of my pledge-brothers will be cleaning Triphammer with a toothbrush tomorrow morning. Does that answer your question? And, by the way, if you see him when you're walking across the bridge, say 'hi,' would you please, and tell him you're my roommate."

"Are you kidding me? That should not be allowed! What's the tuition here? Does this kid's family know that's how he's spending their money?"

"Whose family?"

"Your pledge-brother's."

"Why are you blaming *him*? It's not his fault."

"Okay, then the maniac. I really don't care which one. They're both insane. Your pledge-brother can quit, can't he? He doesn't have to do this."

"Oh yes he does. And only one of them is insane, and everyone in our pledge class knows who that is."

He was mystified that Hal would continue in this pledge program, and stay in this fraternity overpopulated, obviously, with morons. That was hardly his view of Hal and the Cornell demographic. The longer he was on this campus, the more respect he had for the faculty and student body.

He considered calling the office of the Dean of Students, and mentioned that to Hal who got so furious he came close to punching him. What was nuts was that their roles had reversed and Hal was now the one tolerating the most outrageous fraternity stuff. He thought of whistle-blowing anonymously, but Hal might find out who had done it. So he ended up backing off, and rationalizing that it wasn't his problem, that there wasn't anything he could do about it.

He put his energies into his studies, extra efforts even more important this second semester he didn't have Hal as a safety net. Enough with the frats and the social life, he resolved. He was there to get an education. Up the hill, the professors didn't talk of *guts* and *flicks*. They used terms like *gestalt* and *weltanschauung* from the vocabulary of the most elite group of all—the fraternity of scholars. He hunkered down to a routine that would last the remainder of his years on campus. The library, the music room at the Student Union, the deli where he got his coffee and freshly squeezed orange juice, and *Obi*'s diner where he got a late-night *Obi*-burger or omelet. He studied at *all* those places and some unmentionable if he needed *every* minute of the day. He wasn't afraid Paul O'Hara would slam his book down on his desk...but, then again, you never know.

He had no idea anymore what time Hal got to bed; he just knew he couldn't get him up for class in the mornings. By spring they had gone for months barely seeing each other. And on those few evenings Hal showed up in their room before nightfall, his breath was sour from alcohol. When May rolled around, with only three weeks before finals, he ran into Hal on the arts quadrangle.

"Where the hell have you been?" he exclaimed. For the past several nights, Hal hadn't been in his bed at all.

"I got kidnapped!" Hal's speech was slurred and nasal-ized by drink or fatigue, or both.

Michael stood there in a funk, trying to absorb what Hal had just said.

"Tell them just how I busted..." Hal sang from a Cornell fight song to the tune of Give My Regards to Broadway... *lapping up the high, highball.* You wouldn't have seen me in *here,* man," he added, pointing with his thumb, like a hitchhiker, to the library directly behind him, "because I have no intention of taking finals."

This was the first he had heard of the kidnappings, one of the most disruptive of all the pledge pranks, and was shocked by Hal's appearance. The pallor, the beard, the un-combed hair, and the dark circles under his bloodshot eyes seemed to confirm he had pushed the self-destruct button.

"You didn't think your coach could bust out now, did you?"

"Hal, don't screw around like this. What'll your folks say?"

"My folks?" Hal's mouth slanted derisively. "Nothing, man, because they spend all their time and energy talking to the judge. They're in court all day with *Folks v. Folks.* They're splitting!" Hal drew his face in close. His breath felt assaultive.

"Not to worry, Mikey," he added theatrically. "You're the only one who gives a you-know-what."

And then he flipped the hood of his sweatshirt back on his head and walked in the direction of the bridge.

11

WHEN MICHAEL RETURNED to his dorm room late that afternoon, his worst fears were confirmed. He could see easily enough (the closets were alcoves) that Hal's winter coat wasn't there, the alpaca his grandfather, Rupert, had given him. It was a warm day in May, and it made no sense for that coat to be out and about. He opened the center drawer of Hal's desk where he kept his passport, a document he had always viewed with awe because he didn't have one; that wasn't there either. And so it went with the other things that he looked for. Hal had cleared out!

He used the hall phone to call the dorm counselor. Within minutes he got a call back from the Dean of Students office informing him that he no longer had a roommate, that Hal had stopped by the Bursar's Office that afternoon and made the necessary arrangements to leave. The parents, the caller told him, had been informed.

He called Elaine. She answered immediately and, after a minute or so of small talk, he came to the point.

"I'm actually upset!" No sooner were these words out

of his mouth, he began to cry, painfully suppressing every muscle in his body to avoid embarrassing himself in the hall.

Elaine would tell him weeks later she was fearful he had flunked out. When she was a freshman at Michigan, there was a girl in her dorm who went through the school year with great success until finals. She couldn't take her exams because she had lost her memory and whether it was mental or what, Elaine never knew.

"What's wrong?" she asked.

"Hal left."

"*Before* finals?"

"Well, yes. Finals begin in a couple of weeks."

"Do you want me to come there? I can be there tomorrow," she said, a display of loyalty that, in and of itself, helped to calm him.

"No. I'm okay."

"Are you there alone?"

"Yes, I've been alone for months, I mean, he's been practically living at his fraternity. And when he does show up, he's not sober. It's the worst, Elaine. He busted out."

He didn't know why he had said that. Maybe because he still had Hal's voice in his head singing, "tell them just how I busted...."

Elaine was aghast. It had been only a few months since Hal had been with them over Christmas break. To say he was bright and worldly was an understatement. He was amazing. Busting out? Can it be, she wondered?

"Michael, you're not his keeper. He's got parents."

She had a point, he had to admit. It was the random

assignment of a school administrator, wasn't it? He didn't even know Hal eight months ago. That's not a brother. That's an assigned roommate.

"I guess that's right," he said, forcing a chuckle. But as soon as he hung up, this rationale crashed and burned. He pictured how sickly and desperate Hal looked, and then he thought of the bridge. From the time he had come to Cornell, he heard the bridge stories, the students who felt devastated and saw no way out. He felt his stomach tighten and the room get smaller. Everywhere he looked now he saw the things Hal had left—his red wool cap, the reindeer sweater, the electric purple mittens, his white terrycloth robe, the piss yellow parka.

He opened the door, took a deep breath and walked through the hall to the lobby, then out the main entrance in the direction of the fraternity house. They'd be serving dinner in ten minutes. He picked up the pace. The latecomers sat at an extra table halfway out the dining hall. He couldn't have that happen tonight. He needed a seat with his pledge-brothers at their regular table, though he wasn't sure that would help. He didn't know them nearly as well as he knew Hal.

"We found this at the bottom of Triphammer Gorge." Gripping the leash of a large German Shepherd in one hand, and displaying a soiled red shirt in the other, a police officer stood at the door of Michael's room speaking to him, and to Margaret and Mortimer who sat at opposite ends of Hal's bed.

The Hartfields were in the throes of what Hal had called

Folks v. Folks, their vicious divorce proceedings. But when they learned of their son's disappearance, they both rushed up to Ithaca, and not as antagonists. This had united them for the time being, and with surprising civility.

"Does it match the scent of his other clothing?" Mortimer asked.

"Dunno," the officer responded. "That's why I'm here. I need a shirt or something that hasn't been laundered."

"I can tell you that shirt you have there isn't his," said Margaret irritably, though it was her calls to the police department that had prompted the investigation.

The officer looked at Michael, suspecting he would know Hal's wardrobe.

There wasn't a lot to know, Michael reflected. Hal had about four or five shirts, all J. Press stuff, and this one the policeman was holding, fire engine red with a long, pointy collar, wasn't close to belonging.

"She's right, Officer," he said respectfully.

"Well, just the same, I need to check it."

"This is his!" He handed the officer one of Hal's shirts. "It's not that clean, but I guess that's good."

The officer held it to his nose, prompting a twinge. "This will do," he said, and walked out.

They resumed their search through Hal's belongings.

"Look at this," Michael said. He was holding Hal's rush card. "There are a lot of Jewish houses listed here." He handed it to Mortimer.

"Why are these crossed out?" Mortimer asked. He was referring to four fraternities Hal had listed at the top.

"Because he didn't get bids."

"And those were the ones he wanted, obviously," Margaret added. "It's in order of preference."

Hal's chemistry book was lying on the floor. Michael picked it up. Tucked in the front were a couple of folded 8 x 11 sheets of paper with a poem written on it, apparently by Hal. He skimmed it quickly. It was about Rupert Harrison and death, written, it would seem, at the time of the funeral.

"This is about your father," he said, handing the poem to Margaret, who took a few minutes to read it and then passed it on to Mortimer who barely suppressed a scowl. Though Rupert's death had dulled the edges of his bitterness, he wasn't at the point of appreciating encomiums.

In this random way, they leafed through books, papers, and memorabilia for yet another hour, and though there were items of interest like Hal's poem, there was nothing to shed light on his whereabouts. It wasn't until a few days later, after the Hartfields had returned to New York City, that Margaret received a two-sentence letter that had been mailed and postmarked in Chicago, bearing no return address:

Just a note to let you know I'm fine. Not fit for society right now, but I'll call you when I am.

She informed the police who were prepared to analyze the handwriting. That wouldn't be necessary, she told them, that aside from his recognizably poor penmanship, her son often spoke of being fit or unfit for society. At her request, the police brought their investigation to a halt, just hours before they were to initiate a nationwide search of transportation centers and hospitals.

12

THERE WERE ABOUT thirty graduate students waiting in front of the closed door of the seminar room when Michael saw him about ten feet away. Even before he had turned around, he could tell it was Mortimer, the upper torso pitched forward at the waist, the sideburns grayer but, as usual, the head tilted puppet-like to one side.

"I'll be goddamned!" Hartfield said as he walked over. "Michael, you're here?"

"Yes Sir," he responded, knowing instantly that Hartfield was the professor. "I had no idea you were here at Chicago. They didn't have your name in the syllabus."

Hartfield's smile made obvious his suspicion that Michael might not have taken the course had the syllabus been up-to-date.

"I miss my son," he said, his pupils darting to avert Michael's gaze. "Having you in the class will be a joy."

The door of the room opened with a dozen older looking students exiting in intense conversations. And when that had petered out, he and the others waiting pushed in to fill the void. He took a seat near the back. The blackboard was filled with complex equations, what looked like an advanced seminar on logic. Hartfield walked to the front and, with a large chalk eraser, wiped it clean while glancing back a few times to view the students settling into their seats.

"There's room up here," he said, motioning to those in back to move forward. "Let's get cozy, folks. The learning years begin in the womb."

Students chuckled as he motioned for Michael and a woman next to him to move up. And he waited yet another few seconds for that to happen, and then printed his name on the board before clearing his throat to begin.

"Greetings all! I'm Mortimer Hartfield. I'm normally found at Columbia. I had planned on a sabbatical this year but, as you are witnessing, that didn't come to pass."

There was silence in the room, the air charged with the excitement of what had come to pass, some of which had been in the local news and all of which was widely known throughout the Hyde Park community. A couple of months before, philosophy professor Zeno Foufas's wife had been attacked while walking their dog. She was okay, but Foufas was done with Hyde Park, and took a spot at the University of Michigan. It was this act of violence that had brought Mortimer Hartfield to Chicago.

"Anyone who feels cheated because they were expecting Zeno Foufas, feel free to leave now if you like, or, if you wish to be less conspicuous, you may take the proper steps later this afternoon...."

Still talking, Hartfield scribbled furiously on the board. All eyes were on him, and no one would transfer, Michael assumed. A handful of these students knew that Mortimer Hartfield was being modest, that he was Columbia's department chair. And those who didn't know were already impressed by the confidence and outsized ego of the man. For a variety of reasons, he suspected, they would all want to be part of it.

––––––––––––

Back in Chicago for graduate work in philosophy, his life was not as independent as he would have liked. Though he had his own apartment, it was situated so near his father's (where Elaine lived as well), it felt like he was still in the nest. And add to that the constant disapproval. Sam Stein didn't view philosophy as having any practical value. You could make a living as a lawyer or doctor, Sam thought, but not as a philosopher, and upon the mention of almost any subject, he would find a way of bending it to that point.

To minimize these annoyances, Michael avoided discussing anything of substance with his father. When he wanted to share the news about Mortimer Hartfield being his teacher, he called Elaine.

"Guess who I have for a professor," he said.

"Michael, that question's so general. Give me a clue."

"Okay, I'll give you a big, fat clue that you can't miss. Last name begins with H, and he's the father of my freshman roommate. I'm talking about a man I hadn't seen in 3 ½ years, and yet I recognized him instantly from his backside."

"Mortimer?"

There was dead silence. He was confused.

"What is this Mortimer business?" he asked hesitantly. "Do you know Hal's father?"

"I do or I did, yes, but that was, like you said, a long time ago."

"That doesn't make it ancient history. But I know you well enough to know there must be more to this, a lot more. Tell me what this is about, Elaine. I'm not going to get angry. I'm just going to listen."

She cleared her throat. She knew that when her brother said he would not get angry, he already was.

"You don't have to lash out at me like that. It's not appropriate," she said.

"Elaine, please."

"After Hal left Cornell he was headed out to San Francisco, but he got deathly ill on the way. They took him by stretcher from his connecting flight in Chicago and he wound up at Billings. That's how I ended up seeing him. You remember my friend from Michigan—Carole Chin? She was one of his doctors."

"And you never told me this?" He was now moving beyond his own annoyance. Hal deathly ill and he never knew?

"Carole would never tell me anything about her patients. I was respecting that confidentiality, and Hal didn't want anyone to know. That summer after your freshman year, I stopped by her apartment. She wasn't there, but a man answered the door. It took me a moment to realize it was Hal—he was so skinny and his face so pale and drawn—and when it sunk in, I was in shock. That's when I heard the story, that he had just gotten out of the hospital. That he had been in bed for two months!

"Jesus! What was wrong with him?"

"He had a virus that affected a heart muscle. The only cure was just to lie there."

"And so he lay there for two months?"

"Flat on his back. They didn't even give him aspirin because they didn't want to mask the temperature. When weeks later his temperature returned to normal, they knew he was okay."

"Jesus! And I never knew this."

He didn't even tell his parents."

"Where did they *think* he was?"

"They knew he had dropped out of school. But that's all they knew. They had the police investigating."

"I know that. They were in our room."

"When he finally got out after two months of lying in bed, he could hardly walk. Carole invited him to stay at her apartment for a couple of weeks to recuperate. She had an extra bedroom and, besides, she was seldom there. That's where I saw him.

"He called his mother from there—at long last—but didn't say a word about the hospital. She called Mortimer who, it turns out, was three or four blocks away—he was teaching at the U of C that summer—and told him she had heard from Hal and that he was fine. When Mortimer heard this, that Hal had been close-by the whole time, he went ballistic and marched over to Carole's. I was the only one there. At first he thought I was Carole, and after we got that straightened out and he realized who I was, he left, abruptly. He never did see Hal."

Michael heard some muffled sounds at the other end of the phone.

"I never meant to hurt you," she said. She was crying.

"You didn't hurt me. I knew most of this." He was embellishing. "Maybe all of it."

"I have to go now, Michael," she said, still sniffling. "Am I forgiven?"

"Yes. It's over. It's so over, I feel nostalgic."

She laughed, and they said their goodbyes and hung up. He felt relieved to be off. This had gone way beyond what he expected when he made the call. He put on his running shoes. He needed to clear his head, this shocking news about Hal being so ill. Not that it was *his* fault. But he'd have to keep telling himself that, that this had nothing to do with him. It was like walking into a storm. It may be right there in your face, but that doesn't mean it hasn't blown in from a thousand miles away.

————————

"Mr. Stein!"

Mortimer Hartfield peered over the half-moon lens of his reading glasses.

The class sat quietly, all eyes on him now that the professor took issue with the comment he had just made.

"You can't disregard the denotative aspect of the word. It has the same root as a German word that means 'to exit.' We look at what was originally intended to more fully understand how it's currently used."

Hartfield stared at him for a moment as if to ask, "get it?"

This was only the third day of the class, but already he felt over his head. This happened to be a German word

Hartfield had brought into the discussion—one of the four languages the man spoke fluently—but that was only a sampling of his scholarship. There seemed no end to these erudite observations.

After the class adjourned, he was still in the room pulling papers together for his next class when Hartfield walked up to him.

"Michael," he said, his voice thinner and more personal than his stentorian tones in the classroom. "I hope I didn't embarrass you."

He wasn't sure how to respond. Embarrassment wasn't the concern; it was inadequacy.

"You didn't. Don't worry about it, Dr. Hartfield."

"Call me 'Mortimer.'"

"It feels disrespectful...although my sister calls you that apparently."

"How is she?" Hartfield was unfazed.

"Fine." Until he heard his own voice shaking, he hadn't realized how tense he was. "I learned only recently that you two knew each other."

"That seems so long ago now. I went to see Hal at some doctor's apartment as I recall. Your sister was there, but I never did see Hal."

Maybe it was the fact that now *his* voice cracked when he mentioned he "never did see Hal." Whatever the reason, he heard the boy inside the man.

"I'll call you Mortimer."

Over the course of the year he would see a lot of Mortimer Hartfield both inside and outside the classroom. He had taken him down from the pedestal. They were just two guys, he figured, trying to understand life. If during school hours, he was the student and Hartfield was the teacher, in the afterhours they were wine and chess chums killing time together, though he would never ask about Hal. He suspected someone had driven a wedge between those two—Hal and his father—and couldn't possibly have known it was Elaine.

13

THEIR CHESS GAMES were intense and, though they were evenly matched, their styles were very different. Hartfield had textbook strategies while Michael was more casual, playing by instinct or the general principles of battle, he would say. The wine was French, usually a Rhone that Hartfield bought by the case. The deeper discussions didn't begin until they were halfway through a bottle. And then they'd cut loose with all kinds of opinions and theories. A bit tipsy, for sure, with Bach or Beethoven in the background and some bad food to burnish their credentials as ascetics. If the phone rang, they didn't answer. Except on one particular occasion when it wouldn't stop ringing and Michael finally grabbed it.

"Hartfield residence!" he announced, exchanging smiles with Hartfield over his impersonation of a servant.

"Stein sister!" was the response.

"Elaine, is that you?" he blurted out, stretching the phone cord to its fullest as he walked away from where Hartfield was seated.

"Tis I! I'm coming over. I'll bring you a real dinner, if you like. You haven't eaten your rubber pizza yet, have you?"

A large thin box was sitting on the kitchen table. They hadn't yet begun the reheating process.

She knew about the intense chess and the great wine. And from Michael's complaints, she also knew about the hopeless pizza.

"No, not yet. That would be nice," he said.

"I'll be there shortly."

He hung up.

"Who was that?" Hartfield asked. He had been mulling over his move.

"My sister. She's coming over."

"She's coming over?" he exclaimed, looking like he was about to be hit by a bus."

"Yes, and bringing dinner. You can keep this pizza for a late-night snack. Let's try to have at least one meal where you can't complain that the food isn't equal to your wine."

"Well, that's splendid!" he intoned, recovering quickly. "We might elevate this scroungy chess club yet to something more elegant."

Less than a half-hour later she showed up carrying a tray that, through the tinfoil she had covered it with, smelled divine. As she stood at the open door, Hartfield's unease was apparent, making him look more than his fifty years. She, on the other hand, looked radiant, even to her brother who felt like he was seeing her for the first time, now through Hartfield's eyes. With her erect carriage she looked taller than her 5 foot 7 inches, and her lustrous chestnut hair was brushed down to her shoulders. She was not in denim. She wore a skirt Michael hadn't seen before and a white blouse stitched artfully in red that made her look more mature than her years, even a touch matronly as if she had selected it to match up more closely with Hartfield.

"So this is the glamorous side of the family!" Hartfield looked at Michael as if he still needed time to regain his composure. "How are you, Elaine?"

"Fine, Mortimer. It's good to see you again." She walked with her brother to the kitchen while Hartfield returned to the chess table

"You are cooked, my friend!" they heard Hartfield bellow a minute later. He intended the pun.

Elaine's appearance must have stirred his adrenalin because, no sooner had he returned to the chess board, he perceived his path to victory. By the time Michael got there and surveyed the straits his king was in, Hartfield was gloating.

"Dinner's ready!" she announced, snatching Michael from the jaws of defeat.

Hartfield packed the chess pieces away, looking more than satisfied with his undeclared victory and, as he approached the dining room table, could hardly recognize his own dining area. A couple of candles Elaine had lit gave it infinitely more ambience than the overhead chandelier Michael had dubbed the 'pizza light.'

"This, my friend," Hartfield said to Michael, opening another bottle of wine as he was speaking, "will surpass the prior one in both elegance and finish."

He filled a glass for each of them, raising his own in toast. "To Elaine for elevating the culinary standards of our chess club!"

They clinked glasses, but before drinking Mortimer

raised his glass again.

"I shall hold in reserve more specific judgment on the cuisine until the premise has been proved."

She mugged the temperamental chef whose skills were being challenged.

"My dear," said Mortimer ebulliently, "a premise un-proven is like a stallion without...well, let's say, like a geld-ing." He laughed, amused by his own deftness in making the statement less explicit.

As it turned out, she proved the premise, the taste of the food surpassing its presentation. And since the table talk turned to a comparison of James Joyce's and Virginia Woolf's literary techniques, Elaine had the edge. It wasn't only her comparative sobriety (Michael and Mortimer had been drinking for two hours before she arrived). She was on the cusp of her PhD in European literature, and while Hartfield could perform philosophical wonders like reciting Kant by heart in German as well as English, he had only the most basic familiarity with the more contemporary classics of European literature. As the dinner progressed and lit-erature remained the topic, he did less talking and more listening.

Two hours later, Michael left with his sister who drove him to his apartment. Though she was beaming, he had his doubts. The jocularity of the toasts and the coy one-up-manship were only a facade, he suspected, and not where the real feelings dwelled.

———————

Michael liked good food, but his sister's taste buds were those of a gourmet, a continuation of the culinary standards they had become accustomed to as a child. Though most parents give their young children simple, bland foods—kid stuff like peanut butter and jelly, tuna melts and toasted cheese—not Ruth Stein. She served her children complex foods, well seasoned, with fresh vegetables and tasteful sauces. That was her standard and, to her way of thinking, a part of the home.

Sam wouldn't discuss his wife's cooking any more than he would mention the other things that stirred that pain. But when someone served him a delicious dish, his face might register the recognition of this treasured past.

"Now, this is something I haven't had in a long time!" he might exclaim, which his kids took to mean "I haven't tasted anything this good since your mother's cooking."

The corroboration of Ruth's prowess in the kitchen came not only from her husband's tributes and the well developed taste buds of her daughter, but from Sergei and Florence, from cousins on the Harris side, and from Ruth's good friends who, not only savored the product, but had caught glimpses, first-hand, of its production, her hands flying everywhere, so it seemed, slicing, dicing, parsing, rolling, kneading....

Elaine cooked in that tradition. The food she prepared that night for her brother and Mortimer Hartfield could have been one of her mother's recipes. But then again, it could have been her own, or a riff on either or both. It didn't matter. She had the touch...and the flying hands.

14

IT WOULD BE about ten years later (nine, to be exact, after Michael had switched to law from philosophy) that a client of his, a large manufacturing company, was defending a product liability suit and he would get the opportunity once again to see Mortimer. Michael was in New York intermittently for about a month—he wasn't conducting the litigation, only overseeing it—and thus there were periods when time hung heavy on his hands. By late Saturday of his last weekend there, he had signed a settlement agreement with plans to seek final court approval on Monday. Having only one more day in New York, he wanted to see Mortimer while he could still do that conveniently. It wasn't pure nostalgia. There was a subject he had been waiting years to discuss with him.

"Mortimer! A blast from the past!" Michael had called at 9:00 a.m., Sunday, knowing Hartfield was an early riser; he didn't want to miss him.

"Who is this?"

"Michael Stein."

"For God sakes, Michael! How have you been, my good man? To what do I owe this pleasure?"

"To a lawsuit I've been supervising here in the Big Apple. We're going to settle it tomorrow, and then I'll be hopping on a plane.

"Well then I've got to see you *today*," Hartfield said. "Get in a taxi and come over. In the meantime, I'll decide on a good wine. Don't worry. We'll wait for a respectable hour so people won't talk."

It was as if time stood still, Michael reflected, Hartfield speaking so loudly you would think his hearing was impaired. Though he had been divorced for over a decade, he hadn't remarried and, from what Roberta had learned through the grapevine, wasn't currently attached. Clearly, he was delighted with the prospect of Michael's company for the day.

"You look great!" Michael said when he arrived, and he meant it. Indeed he found himself staring at Hartfield, trying to discern one respect in which the man had changed over these past ten years. Was there more gray, a few pounds around the waist, darker circles under the eyes or wrinkles around the mouth? For the life of him he couldn't detect a thing.

"You got here fast," Hartfield said. "That's the good news. The bad news is, I can't break into this wine bottle until Noon. I'll feel I'm a drunk. So let's walk!"

It was a perfect spring day, about 70°, a refreshing breeze and sunny, blue skies. The walk Michael had taken with Hal after that Thanksgiving dinner their freshman year flooded into his consciousness—Hal's criticisms of his father. But on this particular morning, he saw none of those traits, no pomposity. To the contrary, insecurity. The clamminess of Hartfield's palm when they had shaken hands, and the self-conscious way he was gesticulating were the giveaways. This wasn't the vaunted Columbia department chair, the professor with the commanding presence who trained his eyes on you like a searchlight. This was the old wine and chess buddy, the shvitzy one, and it was this conviction that emboldened Michael to break the silence and satisfy his curiosity.

"When you were my professor, I asked you how you came to know my sister. But I never got an answer, not a complete one, at any rate."

"Complete is relative," Hartfield said.

This response irritated Michael and he stopped walking.

"I'd like to know the truth?"

"How *is* Elaine? She's married, is she not?"

"Yes. Why do you ask? She's been married for years, and happily. She has two kids. The oldest one's almost a teenager."

"Then why do you want to know?"

Michael looked confused. "Elaine and I quarreled over that."

"Quarreled over what?"

"That I wasn't told anything at the time. I never knew you were in Chicago, that Hal was ill and in Chicago. I never knew any of it."

"She was keeping her word, preserving a trust," Hartfield said, "an admirable trait all too rare these days. That's nothing to quarrel about. Besides, we were all different then, on our way to becoming, not yet what we are."

"Aristotle?"

"Yes. Don't forget that my son wasn't interested. She had chased after him...all the way to the west coast, and he wasn't interested. Which, to tell you the truth, amazed me, because your sister is a beautiful girl. From the first time I ever saw her, I was struck by her looks...though I must admit I thought she was Hal's doctor, I was in such a snit at the time. The very thought that Hal had been hospitalized all that time right under my nose there in Hyde Park and I never knew it! I was teaching at the U of C that summer. And so when Elaine told me who she was, I was too annoyed to be cordial. I apologized when I called her a month later on the phone to get Hal's phone number. That's when she first told me that she had been with him in San Francisco and stayed at his apartment.

"When I asked her how he was, she said, 'I'm not sure.' Which worried me, and I asked if he had a relapse.

"No, that wasn't what she meant, she said. She just couldn't figure him out.

"I told her I had *never* been able to figure him out, not since the time he was born. And when I got a hearty laugh from that line, I asked if I could take her to dinner. I know I surprised her with that invitation. She hesitated a moment before she accepted. I picked her up that evening at her apartment and we went to a restaurant a few blocks away. From the time we sat down, all we did was talk about Hal. I hadn't asked her out to talk about my son. But when I tried to change the subject, she got even more determined and asked me if there was something about Hal she didn't know.

"Like what? I asked.

"'Well,' she said, 'this may sound egotistical, but he showed no interest in me.'

"I didn't know *what* to say. The relationship had originally been platonic, you know. When you guys hung out together that Christmas in Chicago, I'm told, she was one of the guys, shooting pool. And while platonic can become romantic, of course—it happens all the time—there's usually some defining event and that apparently never occurred.

"She thought he was gay—she had that much self-confidence—but I knew that wasn't the case. So when she said he showed no interest, I just brushed it off with something suggestive. As I said, I hadn't asked her out to talk about my son. And she wasn't one of *my* students, so as far as I was concerned there were *no* ethical issues. She was 23, a consenting adult. When Margaret was 23, Hal was three years old. So, rest assured, Elaine was of age. This was nothing inappropriate, much less illicit. Our relationship was the natural intersection of our two lives—for that time and place."

Back at his apartment, Hartfield opened the wine bottle. Michael was the one who needed the drink. His head was spinning from this Hartfield universe with its own set of rules. They talked about a lot of things that afternoon before he left—philosophy, the law and the litigation he was concluding, but never another word about Elaine. And he was okay with that. Because if he never got the full story it wouldn't change anything. How could it? When what happened between them—Mortimer and Elaine—was for that time and place only.

———————

The time: a scorchingly, hot evening in July, 1968. The place: Hyde Park. The dramatis personae: Mortimer Hartfield, teaching at the University of Chicago that summer, and our heroine, Elaine Stein, who had just returned from two weeks of unwanted chastity in San Francisco. The situation: an after dinner drink at his apartment on the third floor of a walk-up, an ascent that proved challenging, so wasted was she from the wine at dinner.

"You do this every day?" she asked, marveling at Hartfield's brisk pace a few stairs ahead of her.

"I do, but it's not usually this hot. I need some air!" he exclaimed after reaching the top and entering the apartment. He proceeded to the living room where he opened two large windows, then sat down on the couch, took off his tie, and tossed it on the coffee table.

She took a seat on a large soft chair opposite the couch and table. The cotton sweater she had worn in the restaurant felt like an overcoat. It was about 85 degrees outside and hotter than that in this upstairs apartment with no cross ventilation. The nights had been like this for almost a week now, hotter and more still than the day.

She removed her sweater and placed it alongside his tie, the familiarity of this arousing to Hartfield, who stared at her breasts through her sheer, silk turtleneck.

"Would you like some wine?" he asked.

"Just some water," she replied, but without conviction, and since an after dinner drink was ostensibly her reason for this visit, Hartfield brought her some port wine along with the water she had requested.

"You have them both, my Dear," he said, setting them on the coffee table in front of her. "That's a 20-year port. It'll go down easier than the water."

And within the next couple of minutes they emptied their wine glasses. Though he was unaffected, she was even more wasted.

The phrase "wasted," in this context, would seem to connote a lack of sobriety, and so at this point assume Elaine Stein might throw caution to the winds. After all, that had been his hope when he invited her to join him on the couch, an invitation that a more sober woman might have declined.

"Why the turtle neck in these tropics?" he asked, as she settled into a spot next to him.

"Did you want me to add it to the pile?" she asked, gesturing comically, her hand landing on the erect male member sprouting from his crotch.

She pulled back quickly. "I'm sorry," she said, embarrassed.

"That's quite alright," he said unflappably. "It's my fault. I expanded into your space."

And now, high and silly, they both smiled.

He poured her another glass of the port. She didn't protest.

"I'm not as unappreciative of your body...and your beauty, as my son."

He leaned to kiss her and she met his lips with hers.

"This mock turtle neck is mocking me," he said.

"That's not polite," she said, taking yet another swig of the port. And with a highly practiced motion, crossed her arms and pulled off the gauzy veil that Hartfield had already lifted in his imagination.

She leaned back on the couch. He threw his shirt and trousers to the side and pulled her panties down from under her skirt, past her feet. Then tried to penetrate but couldn't.

He sat up, calmly rolling on a lubricated condom he had

extracted from his wallet.

"Relax, my love, and we'll have a lovely time."

And with that he moved her through it, up and down and around until she cried out with joy, and he too, a moment later, unloosed his pleasure.

"You're a real woman now," he said in the aftermath, bestowing a light kiss upon her lips, as if it were congratulatory.

And indeed she was pleased. She had always thought this moment would be awkward or physically painful or ill timed or all of the above. But not so, and after sleeping for maybe thirty minutes, she awakened with a resurgent longing. This stirring awakened him, and while the amount of wine Hartfield had consumed might have limited the ambitions of most men, he proved capable of repeat performances in different positions and venues until the wee small hours of the next day when she took a cab back to her apartment, a true graduate student.

It was too good to not repeat in the weeks that followed—three weeks to be exact—by the end of which time she had come to her senses. Those rebuffs by Hal now a fading memory, and her concerns mounting that, the condoms notwithstanding, she'd get pregnant, she called it quits like a chain smoker who's tossed her cigarettes away. Fact was, she had become increasingly removed, fantasizing during the act itself that her lover was the son rather than the father. Their shared destiny had passed. He was middle-aged, divorced, a father, and a lover to numerous other women around the globe. She was 23, looking for a man in her life, hoping for marriage and dreaming of children. Rationally it wasn't a match. And by any reckoning, it wasn't love.

Book Two
Hal

15

HE WATCHED THE car pull into the driveway.

"Someone's here!" Hal exclaimed.

His 10-year old daughter jumped for joy. "I'll get my stuff!" she shouted, referring to the bag he had packed for her with a bathing suit and sweatshirt.

"It's not Judy," he said when he was able to see more closely the make and color of the car. And with that he heard the front doorbell, and opened it. My God, he thought, he looks great, overwhelmed that it had been almost 20 years since he had seen him.

"Michael!" he exclaimed, giving him a bear hug.

"Zoe, sweetheart, this is Michael. He was my best friend at school. Like you and Judy, we did everything together."

Zoe looked their guest over. "Nice to meet you," she said begrudgingly, the verdict clear that Michael was not on a par with Judy.

Hal had released the bear hug and was now gripping Michael by the arm.

"Saturdays, we always do something together, but because you're our special guest today, Michael, we've changed our schedule. Zoe's going to her friend Judy's house. She won't be suffering. Their pool is nicer than ours."

As he looked at his daughter to confirm that she would hold up her end of the bargain, a car appeared and Zoe's attention transferred to her friend in the back seat. By the time Hal and Judy's mother had chatted, and she had exchanged pleasantries with Michael, the two girls were in full giggles. After they drove off, the silence was deafening.

"Well, that's a bundle of joy," Michael said, as he followed Hal to the patio where their swimming pool was located.

"I hate that girl," he replied.

"I know. I can tell."

Hal sat on a colorful, thickly cushioned chaise, Michael taking one across from him

"So tell me about this case that brings you to L.A."

"Well, this particular one is not that interesting. Honestly, if it weren't for the opportunity to see you, I would have sent an associate."

"That's the advantage of having your own firm, isn't it?"

"One of the small advantages, yes."

"I can see this agrees with you, Michael. Your firm, your family. You look great!"

He sat silently, regretting he couldn't sincerely return the compliment. He had had one of his clients who does background checks for corporations, run a search on Hal. This was a beautiful house, but this he also knew: it hadn't been easy for his old roommate and that was evident—

physically. Hal looked older than his years.

"I have the feeling my life has been boring and conventional compared to yours," Michael responded, eager to acknowledge Hal's apparent success.

"Well, I'm not sure about that," Hal said. "But if that means it's my turn to talk, hang on for a minute. I'll be right back." And while it was more than a minute, it wasn't a whole lot longer than that when he returned with two frozen lattes topped with whipped cream.

"I guess it's my turn now," he said, good-naturedly. "Where do I begin?"

"At the beginning, when you left Cornell."

"I'm not sure you want all the details. I was a sick boy."

"Actually, I got the details from Elaine. I was pretty upset that I hadn't been told anything about it at the time."

"That's my fault. I was very hyper about keeping it secret. Kept a lot of things secret in those days, like the fact that I had a cocaine addiction, and was married to the manager of the dry cleaners where I worked. Though we couldn't keep the marriage secret after she was pregnant. Which turned out to be what saved me, because Mary— that was her name—had the better job and so I quit working to take care of the baby. I had the time then to go to AA meetings—for the cocaine, not booze—and, if you can believe it, even went to church on Sundays. That's how hard I tried, and I kicked the habit. To this day, I won't have even a beer.

"With my Mr. Mom routine I signed up for some correspondence courses and, though it wasn't at a Cornell level, for the first time in my life I felt motivated to do some serious studying. A year and a half later, Mary filed for divorce. We had no property except the trust fund my Grandpa Rupert had set up for me, and that wasn't anything she could get her hands on. So it was all very simple. Before I knew it, we had signed some releases and we were done. She took off with Zoe—she had gotten exclusive custody because of my cocaine history—and though she was required under the court order to tell me where she was going, she didn't. She lied; threw out some phony address. I should have called the police, but I was the one with the criminal record, and I felt vulnerable.

"Thank God, I didn't fall back on the habit," he said, setting his jaw. "I had been studying hard before Mary and I split, and afterward worked harder than ever. A spotless personal record including strong academics, I had been advised, would enhance my chances to share custody of Zoe. After being accepted into the graduate Psychology program at UCLA, I made an appointment with my attorney to begin pursuing joint custody. And it was only a couple of days later that I got the call from the police department in Boston that Mary was dead. Her neighbor, who was babysitting Zoe, had been calling the hospital and the police to inquire about relatives.

"I would never have wished Mary dead, but I'd be lying if I didn't admit I was ecstatic to get my daughter back. Within two hours, I was on a plane to Boston to pick her up. After a connection in Chicago, I arrived late in the evening, got a few hours sleep at one of the airport hotels that night, and then early the next morning set out to get her. It was an older section of Brookline with small, charming homes. Mary had leased a basement apartment and Marjorie, the woman she had relied on for childcare, lived in the house directly across the street. Her husband was a doctor at one of the Boston hospitals. She had a daughter, Carlie, who was Zoe's age.

"My heart beat like crazy when I walked in. Marjorie introduced herself, and was classy enough to express her condolences though, for all she knew, I was a bitter ex-husband. It felt strange to meet her, this woman who was more familiar with my daughter than I was. I found myself taking in all her mannerisms, her broad New England 'A's, her sense of style, the way she moved her hands, all the things I assumed had made an impression on my daughter. I was struck by her appropriateness, as she checked my identity in a polite but thorough way. My initial feeling at that moment was one of relief that Mary, whose judgment I had always thought so flawed, had found this impressive person to take care of Zoe. I followed her to the rear, sunny section of her house where the girls were in the playroom.

"I knew in an instant who was who, though Carlie was not that dissimilar looking. It's just that Zoe had that Hartfield energy, as if she had to do at least two things at once. She was writing the alphabet, holding the pen and cocking her head like a writer, while singing some song that was in her head with a pitch I knew (from when she was eighteen months old) was perfect. The sun, shining brightly through the windows, beamed right on Zoe's little face. It was as if the other little girl was no longer in the room.

"Maybe it was the sun in her eyes, because she didn't seem to recognize me. She was a baby and a tiny tot when she had been with me, and so I had expected to not be recognized. But when it actually happened, my excitement turned to despair. Mary had worked such long hours at the cleaners that Zoe and I had been joined at the hip from morning to night, an extremely happy eighteen months of my life. And now here in front of me, again, in this home in Boston, was the light of my life who was three and a half years old, and all I could think of was the two precious years I had lost.

"I tried for several minutes to make contact, a few silly faces I used to do, even a couple of nursery rhymes like Old King Cole and Wee Willie Winkie that I used to sing for her back then. She looked up with a confused expression, and then dug even deeper into the letters she was trying to write. Marjorie and I shared an expression of futility. It was then that she so brilliantly intervened. She explained to Zoe that I was her daddy and that I loved her and missed her and wanted to take her home with me, because her mommy wasn't going to be coming back, but that if Zoe preferred, she could come home with her and Carlie. It was pure bluff, because Marjorie had been desperate to be relieved of this responsibility. And, as I said, it turned out to be the most brilliant of strategies because that was all Zoe had to hear. She started to cry and when Marjorie came over to console her, she wailed even louder. Abandoning all caution, I hugged her tightly and, reaching into my wallet, pulled out a Band-Aid, which is what I would do sometimes when I used to take care of her.

"She looked at it as if she were trying to remember where this came from and then she said, using words I had taught her back then, 'I don't have a boo-boo.' She stopped crying and I showered her with kisses.

"We've been joined at the hip again ever since." He paused. "I give Mary credit for giving Zoe the stability and independence to go with me that day. It may be mental gymnastics, but when I think of that failed marriage now I think that something wonderful came out of it. I deeply regret that her life ended so brutally. She had her problems, certainly, could lie, cheat and steal, the effects of her harsh upbringing. But she never drank, couldn't stand the smell of alcohol. And it was a drunk driver crossing the median strip that killed her head-on."

At Pacific Valley Dry Cleaners, where he and Mary worked, the employees were all immigrants, so frugal they would dunk day-old donuts and drain their saucers into their cups to get the last drop from their fifteen-minute coffee break. He admired them for their old-world work ethic, their cheerfulness in the face of drudgery. They were of European ancestry, mostly Scotch and Irish, people who in a previous generation would have risen at the break of day and spent that day outside driving their sheep to market. While here, inside the chemical laced walls of the dry cleaning plant, their days were enlivened by coffee breaks.

Not that his admiration for them was returned; it wasn't. The fact that he drove to work made him an object of envy to these employees who relied on public transportation. Forget that he had paid only a $100 for his used car, a two-door Ford with almost 100,000 miles and lots of dents. The fact that he had a car (and paid the insurance premiums), that he was dating the manager (they didn't know they were married), that he was born in the U.S. and was raised in Manhattan, all of these things distinguished him as surely as if he had spoken the King's English to a Cockney East Ender.

Beyond that, though, there was a more serious cause for distrust. He had been to college, one of the employees learned—an Ivy League school no less (forget that he didn't last a year)—which made it official that he was not one of them, that they knew very little about him, that he didn't seem to work as hard as they (though he did), that he didn't pour the coffee from his saucer back into his cup (guilty as charged), that he wore a warm, expensive looking Alpaca coat (the birthday gift from his Grandpa Rupert), and that

he had toured the countries they came from. He didn't belong.

His whole personal history, as we know, was one of not
belonging. The free-thinking, atheistic father who scorned
religion and, for that matter, any categorical identification.
The mother to the manor born, isolated by the wealth and
fame of her family. The Grovener preppies who enjoyed
the company of their roommates while he was alone in his
single. The fraternities that divided the world into Jew and
gentile, and threw him into the latter category when his
own heart and closest friend was in the former. And now
here at Pacific Valley Dry Cleaners, the Ellis Island alums
who spurned the college boy.

"We're going to have a detective here today and maybe
tomorrow, and I need all of you to cooperate."

These were the words of the owner at a meeting of all
personnel that had been called to alert them to a problem
concerning a missing garment. It was a powder blue cashmere sweater embroidered with rubies, and the customer
would not accept cash to cover the loss. She wanted her
sweater, and had contacted the police department. For the
next week, the staff wallowed in distrust. Everyone was the
object of suspicion, it seemed, except him. He wasn't sure
what had insulated him. Maybe it was the Ivy League aura.
Or his Alpaca coat? Or perhaps a general refinement that
made it implausible that he might be the thief. After a day
and a half, the detective left. He hadn't a clue.

Shortly after that, Zoe was born, and he would be leaving his job at the cleaners to take care of her.

"You look after yourself, Laddie," one of his fellow employees said, a middle-aged woman who had developed a
real affection toward him.

Things had changed in that respect. She wasn't the only one. A couple of the other women along with one of the men, all Scottish immigrants, had begun to take him under their wing. The feelings they had earlier of his being a privileged college kid were beside the point now. It wasn't because they learned he never completed a year. The change in their attitude stemmed from the way he handled himself during the time the detective was there. He was supportive and empathetic, and made that difficult period of their employment more tolerable. And now they were genuinely sorry to lose him. For his final coffee break in the cafeteria, they treated him to coffee and a chocolate doughnut.

"Your money's no good here, Hal," one of the women told him when he tried to pay.

He was touched. He knew how frugal they were.

Eighteen months later, Mary quit. They were divorcing. Their apartment was strewn with bags, as she packed up Zoe's and her belongings to take Zoe off to the mystery location she wouldn't truthfully disclose. His main concern at that time was that Mary not forget anything essential to Zoe. He had been her primary caregiver and knew better than she the constellation of stars that Zoe needed so all would be right in the universe. As he checked the closets, he found Zoe's Baby Girl on the floor, the beloved doll that had been the first word out of her mouth. He brought it over to Mary's large suitcase. Surely, he thought, he could find some room in there for Baby Girl. He opened the case.

"Exactly what do you think you're doing?" Mary growled as he looked up at her. She was standing over him.

"Putting the doll in here," he answered. "I didn't think it merited a big negotiation."

"I was planning on taking it," she said, "but I'm not put-

ting it in there. Now I'll thank you to close my suitcase." She held out her hand for the doll.

He handed it to her and then closed her suitcase, but not before seeing, partially beneath a couple of sheer panties, a powder blue cashmere sweater embroidered with rubies.

The patio area, where he and Michael were sitting, was elegantly landscaped.

"Is it your wife who has the sense of aesthetics?" Michael asked.

"We've got great landscapers," he replied, "and I find some time, now and then, to give it that personal touch, but Colette, no! She's never home."

"What does she do?"

"Teaches history at UCLA. And spends a lot of time traveling. She's on the executive board of the National Association of History Professors. Irony of ironies. I fled to California to be with an intense professor again...a Dr. Hartfield, no less."

Michael smiled. "You're sitting with someone who knows of the doctor fetish."

"That's true, Hal said, conspiratorially. "But let me clarify that while Colette does have a PhD, no one calls her Doctor. She's plain old Professor Hartfield."

"And who was she before she was a Hartfield?"

"Well, you remember my telling you about my summer in Paris before my last year at Grovener. That's the girl! My wife. Fortunately for me, she didn't hold my youthfulness against me. Twenty years later she moved to the states and

accepted a position at UCLA where I was an adjunct professor. Her parents had died, and she had been married
and divorced in France, with no children. So in this strange
way our lives had intersected again, and this time we got
it right."

"You were lucky."

"I was. She's amazing." And then he added what he always said when he thought of the blessing of Zoe. "And I
was lucky in a different way the first time around.

"Colette's not the stepmother type," he added. "She and
Zoe couldn't be closer. In fact, it's irritating as hell when
they gang up on me, but I wouldn't want it any other way."

For a moment, neither spoke.

"And your work?" Michael asked. "I've gotten the feeling in our phone calls that it's something you care about
very deeply."

"Well, you knew me when I didn't care much about anything. But, yes, this I'm passionate about. Like I told you, it
all started when I was home with Zoe...and then when she
was taken from me. That was the first time in my life I gave
it my all."

"And you had a lot to give. That I know."

"Well, thank you. I didn't exactly squeak by. I graduated
first in my class, and had a PhD in two years. Am I brag-
ging?"

"Yes, but to the right person, because it's nice to know
I was proved right. You were the most able student I ever
knew."

Hal swallowed hard, out of pride. It meant a lot to him
to hear this praise from Michael.

"I taught and did clinical work for about five years. And

then one day I was home sick and happened to pick up an old paperback I had bought and read years before—Vance Packard's *The Hidden Persuaders*. Started me thinking about the impact psychology can have on marketing and advertising. Next thing I knew, I took some Grandpa Rupert trust money I had saved, and I rolled the dice on a new business. It's been going well. It's based on a program we offer to evaluate customer satisfaction in advertising, but in a very different way from what had traditionally been done. It's more behavioral."

They talked for another couple of hours, had a late lunch, and then around 4:00 p.m., Zoe returned from her play-date, bounding joyfully into her father's arms. Michael was charmed.

"She was my other inspiration for starting the business," Hal said after she had excused herself to do her weekend homework.

Seeing a skeptical look on Michael's face, he added, "I'm serious, she really was. I would watch her in the playroom while I did my work. You know, with kids and their play, you can tell if it captures their imagination. It's not in the noise they make. It's in the quiet."

He stood up, then paced back and forth.

"The Hartfield Program—that's what we call it—evaluates experiential data, buying patterns. It's a lot different from traditional customer surveys. Those get easily distorted. In a typical survey, the answers you get reflect the mood of the customer at the moment of sampling. Think of a call, for example, when a mother is trying to put her children to bed; her answers will reflect impatience. And that doesn't take into account the mothers who won't take the call under those circumstances. Those are the kinds of distortions that skew the data. You see...."

A chip off the old block, Michael reflected. Hal could talk about this all day. For Mortimer, it was the great masters of philosophical thought, and now for the son, a psychology-based business system. But for both, it was about thinking creatively.

The airport limo arrived. While Hal ran upstairs to get Zoe to say goodbye, Michael poked around the living room, intrigued by its informality, storage drawers hidden in each of the four corners, stuffed with toys and games, movies like the Wizard of Oz, and other children's stuff. You wouldn't know that by just glancing at the room, and you wouldn't have noticed the video projector concealed behind a sliding panel of the coffee table, or the motorized drop-screen recessed in the ceiling.

A few minutes later he was waving to Hal and Zoe as the limo pulled out of the driveway. Then, resting his head against the back seat, Michael allowed himself a moment to savor the joy and satisfaction of this visit. He had come there presuming Hal's life would be so different, and yet it all felt so similar: a strong marriage; the deep love between parent and child; professional and business achievements one could own and be proud of, these and the other aspects of their lives they shared. He had come to California to take a deposition. But if he had also come in search of a common denominator with his roommate of years ago, he had found that too in the hidden playroom of this ranch house in Santa Monica.

————

When he was 17, Hal's mother decreed that he would learn French as she had, by living in France for the summer, a plan he welcomed after three years in his single at Gro-

vener. On his voyage over, he struck up a friendship with another boy in the program, Robert Morgan from Philadelphia, who like him had roots in old money, withholding parents and a snobby prep school. When they disembarked at Le Havre, they were shuttled by van to Paris and the Sorbonne where he and Morgan (they chose to be roommates) threw their suitcases into the small Renault of their host, Madame Montrecoeur, and were on their way.

"My daughter will be waiting there," Madame had told them, this comment having no effect until they arrived and Morgan spotted the daughter, his eyes bulging with desire.

"Do you see what I see, bub?" he asked, spoofing a British accent. "And not jail bait either!" Morgan was counting on the advance information he had received that Madame spoke no English.

Colette Montrecoeur, age 20, stood around five-seven, had flaming red hair, a heart-shaped face, green eyes set widely beneath dark, thick lashes, a Roman nose and ruby lips that had no need of lipstick. She was standing in front of the apartment building, waving to her mother to take the parking space in front of the door. And if her sexy looks and voice weren't enough, Morgan's frenzy would be further fueled by the fact that the guest room for their stay was ordinarily her bedroom.

"You understand, Hal," Morgan said, rummaging around the room ecstatically, "that this pillow had her head on it, and these sheets...oh my God..." he exclaimed, " I'm getting hard."

His eyes rolled around in his head as he struggled to process this, his weeks of advance planning, the eight-day transatlantic crossing, and his own expectations for the summer now subordinated to Morgan's infatuation with Colette Montrecoeur. He threw some soap and water on his face and came out to their small dining room where they were joined for lunch, as was the daily custom, by Madame's husband, Monsieur Montrecoeur, who owned a small wine shop that he closed for a couple of hours at noon.

"Tell me," Monsieur asked Morgan once they were seated and eating, "about your family and where you live."

Always curious about the backgrounds of their guests, Monsieur got more than he bargained for as Morgan marched though his family history, their early roots in manufacturing, and the more recent progeny of socialites. By the time it was Hal's turn to talk, he was determined to produce a background less privileged.

"My father is a professor," he said, his French virtually free of an accent. "He spends his time teaching and studying. My mother's family, has a business that I would guess is not unlike yours, Monsieur, in the sense that it requires a constant effort to keep moving it forward." (And in such a manner was a railway empire equated to a neighborhood wine shop).

Deflating the Harrison legacy was only a part of his plan. Hanging around when Colette was there was more strategic. While Morgan partied, Hal remained at the Montrecoers in his room studying where he would seek, more often than was necessary, Colette's help for a translation or pronunciation. She was always there, studying for the baccalaureate. And then in the afternoon, after they both felt deserving of a break, they might bike for a few miles where they would sit and chat before heading back for dinner.

They spoke in English. It was simply that they were engaged in intense discussions, and thus language served its primary purpose as a means of communication, her English vocabulary much larger and more nuanced than his in

French. This was their little secret because Madame Montrecoeur, scrupulous about observing the foreign exchange students' contract, would have been furious with Colette. Though not nearly as furious as she would have been had she known there was more to these bike rides than the fresh air and exercise.

Madame could never have imagined that her 20-year old daughter would have a romantic interest in a 17-year old schoolboy. There wasn't anyone she knew who had that kind of relationship, and though she had only to see the interracial couples strolling along the Seine to know that love draws its own boundaries, crossing this age divide seemed to her improbable. No less improbable, by the way, than it seemed to Hal. He had his hopes, of course, but most often it felt like a pipedream. Colette had so thoroughly spurned Morgan, she had driven the lad to drink it appeared. And while Hal had gone through contortions to differentiate himself as the scholarly and industrious one, love has a more ineffable quality, so elusive to capture.

One afternoon three weeks into the summer, when Morgan was off decorating a room for one of his parties, and Monsieur and Madame were not expected home until 8:00 P.M., Hal returned to the apartment after his last class where he bumped into Colette who was the only other one there. Though she had greeted him numerous times—in the morning, afternoon and evening—this encounter with no one else at home felt different and intimate, and they both blushed.

"My parents have gone to a wake," she said in French. "They'll be home around 8:00." He knew that, and more awkwardly she knew he knew that.

They also knew where Morgan was, getting ready for his party, because he had been talking about that for the past several days.

"Where is it that your parents have gone?" he asked, not knowing the French word for "wake."

And after she repeated it, using the English word, he teased her about her pronunciation in which the "w" sounded like a "v," drawing his face closer to hers and pursing his lips like a Frenchman to tease out his imitation. Suddenly, impulsively, she stopped him with her own lips—on his!

He stood there dumbly, and had he not been so surprised, he would have just grabbed her.

She smiled mischievously as if to say, "Don't you know, you dope, that I'm crazy about you."

But the moment had passed. And her smile faded, not out of shame (she didn't feel that), but rather to acknowledge that she owned that kiss, and that it wasn't an impulse.

"You ought to do that more often when I run on at the mouth," he said, resorting to cheekiness, any greater daring having failed.

It would still be light out for a few hours. Instinctively they knew the only way of diffusing this was to escape outside. They went for a bike ride. Within a half-hour they were in the environs on a quiet, deserted path they knew well. They stopped to share the water bottle mounted on Colette's bike. As she drank, he drew close to her, as if he were impatient to get some for himself. As she released the bottle, this time he was the one whose lips closed in on hers.

They collapsed to the ground, their arms entwined. She popped open the top button of his Jeans. He was hard, harder, he felt, than he had ever been before. He reached round her back to unclasp her bra as she pulled his briefs below his hips, his member now pulsing hot against her hand before it throbbed wildly and erupted, viscous wads wasting on the black, dirt path of the trail. Her face flushed red. He lay there confused.

"We'd better get back now," she said, as if a genie had been let out of the bottle. They stood up and zipped and buttoned and adjusted their clothing.

When they arrived home, her parents were there, Madame explaining that she had remembered Morgan's party and wanted to serve dinner early so they (Colette and Hal) wouldn't miss it. Colette, all sweaty and with eyes redder than usual, went straight to her room.

There were other opportunities that summer that he and Colette had to consummate their desires. But so powerful was the impulse, they steered clear of it certain they were on the edge of disaster. Three weeks later, Madame and Colette took him and Morgan to the train station, a sad and quiet ride, even Morgan uncharacteristically tongue-tied except for a clumsy comment about Colette having her bed and bath back to herself. As for Hal, who would board a ten-day steamer for Montreal and go by rail to New York, Pennsylvania and Grovener, it would be years before it would surface again, the special destiny of this unfulfilled love.

16

"ARE YOU ALRIGHT, Sir?"

He was at the gate at Midway, getting his seat assignment for his flight to San Francisco.

"I'm not sure." Sweating profusely and unsteady on his feet, Hal was finding it difficult to believe this was just nerves, the stress of dropping out of school. There was a long line of impatient people behind him. She let him board. It happened that his seat was next to a physician who couldn't help but notice him shivering.

"Do you have a fever, young man? I'm a doctor."

His teeth had begun chattering, and now his whole body was trembling.

"I don't think so," Hal replied hesitantly, but as soon as he had said this, he began to perspire again profusely despite the blowing from the little vents above him.

"I don't think you should be leaving here, Son," the doctor said.

Hal slumped over, trying to quell his shivers by pressing his body against the back of the seat. He heard the engines rev up and hoped the doctor didn't say anything that would keep him from staying on the plane.

"We should take your temperature."

It was then that he began to shake uncontrollably. And when a flight attendant appeared a moment later and told him to sit upright and fasten his seat belt for takeoff, he couldn't.

"This young man is in no condition to take this flight," the doctor said to the startled flight attendant.

"Sir?"

"I'm a doctor," he said. "This boy is seriously ill! He needs medical attention immediately."

"Yes Doctor!" She walked quickly up the aisle in the direction of the cockpit.

A half-minute later, the engines were shut down and the pilot came down the aisle. The only part of it Hal remembered was that the pilot wasn't walking fast enough. Five minutes later he was carried out on a stretcher while a little boy asked loudly "Is he dead?"

An ambulance rushed him to an emergency room at Elmhurst Hospital where his high temperature of 108°, coupled with an abnormal EKG, confounded the medical staff. Just when he began convulsing and his condition looked critical, the fever began to break. By 6:00 a.m., Elmhurst transported him by helicopter to Billings Hospital at the University of Chicago.

His fever more manageable by then, he was able to provide the doctors with information, including his activities during the period leading up to his illness. The precipitating cause was a hazing activity which his pledge-master had dubbed "The Abe Lincoln." It entailed splitting a small log into toothpicks, which took hours of laborious work with a hatchet, made more hazardous by a prohibition against touching the log. Weary from flailing at the leaping log, he gashed his leg. There wasn't much blood, and that's what threw him off at the time; the hatchet had chopped into his Tibia,. He went to the on-campus clinic where they cleaned and dressed the wound, and told him to keep an eye on it. In his distracted state, he never changed the pad and so he never saw the bright colors it turned before settling into something ominously pus-filled. By the time Michael saw Hal for the last time on the Arts Quadrangle, a serious infection was brewing, only one of the reasons he looked so terrible.

The rest has been told—the airport, ambulance, stretcher, helicopter, delirium, and the cadre of physicians trying to comprehend this sudden deterioration of a sturdy 19 year old. As he lay there at Billings, his condition stabilizing with an antibiotic drip, the consensus formed among his attending physicians that he had two different problems—a staph infection from the hatchet gash, and a viral Myocarditis, an inflamed heart muscle. And while the staph infection was expected to subside within the week, the heart muscle could remain inflamed for a couple of months, a monitoring and recovery period that in those days required absolute bed rest and hospitalization.

It was near the end of his first week at Billings that Carole Chin came into the picture, and gave him books to read which they'd discuss. And when he learned that she had gone to the Lab School, he asked her if she knew Michael Stein.

"I knew a Stein at Michigan," she said, as she pressed a stethoscope to his back. "But that's a common name, I know."

"No," he said. "He didn't go to Michigan."

"Elaine. Elaine Stein," she said. "That's who I'm talking about."

"Wait!" he blurted out. "Elaine Stein? That's his *sister*."

"Are we talking about the same Elaine Stein?" she asked. "Kind of tall? About five foot seven? Brown hair. Very pretty."

He was miserable at physical descriptions. Though he had lived with their family that Christmas vacation, he couldn't picture her height or hair color.

"Maybe." He thought for a couple of seconds and then an image of Elaine finally came into focus. "Yes. I'm sure of it, yes."

"We're good friends," said Carole. "Like I said, we were at Michigan together. She's a graduate student now in European literature here in the Chicago area."

"That would be her," he said. "She was very serious about literature."

She balled up her stethoscope and slid it into the large pocket of her three-quarter length white jacket. Their relationship had deepened; he knew her good friend.

"Don't say anything," he said.

"I never mention my patients." Then she smiled as if to signal she was off record. "So her brother Michael is a friend of yours?"

He told her all about the dorm, the fraternity, his parents, the divorce, his whole life it seemed. It was as if she had hit the jackpot at a slot machine. She was so deeply into it that one of the attending physicians had to stick his head in and give her a hint to move on. And when she finally did leave, he felt more alone than ever with his unresolved feelings and the dangling parts of this narrative he had unfolded.

––––––––––––

Though he was hospitalized the entire month of July displaying his elusive myocardial rub to curious medical students, the time passed quickly, so consuming did he find the literature Carole Chin had supplied, and the discussions he had with her. He had never been in an environment as conducive to study and contemplation as this sterile hospital room, barren except for the bed, a chair, and a wall-mounted black and white TV he never watched. During his childhood, his father would spend hours in their wood paneled library, lined with books while he and his mother and everyone else in the house tiptoed around trying not to disturb the great one at work. But real thought and contemplation, he was to learn that summer, can be had in the unlikeliest places if you're up for it, because at no time in his life did he do more serious reading and thinking than in this hospital with noises and interruptions beginning at the earliest hours of the morning when they would come in to check his "vitals."

"You can stay at my place for a while. I have an extra bedroom." Carole Chin said.

It was the end of August and, at long last, he was being discharged. However, his legs had atrophied and he couldn't stand for long, or walk distances.

"It would be the smart thing to do," she added, "before going on to the west coast."

"Are you sure that's not a problem?"

"A problem? I'm hardly ever there. When I'm not at the hospital, I'm at my fiancé's."

He took her up on it, enjoying at first the quiet environment for his reading, though after a few days he missed the intrusiveness of the hospital staff. He had decided it was too solitary by the time Elaine Stein dropped by.

"I can't believe it!" she exclaimed. "You look so different! So much older!" She was blushing. "But I mean in a good way." Which wasn't exactly the truth because, while she was delighted to see him, she was shocked by how pale and thin he was.

"You've been doing a lot of reading, Carole tells me." She teased out the word *reading*. "Like what?"

A question that hung in the air, it was so awkwardly specific considering they had just re-acquainted seconds before. A matter of trying too hard, undoubtedly, because she hadn't dated much, a fact and condition that had begun to dominate her life. And if her father asked her each day what her evening plans were, and she didn't have any, that was just a minor irritant. Marriage was the big worry, not here and now, but being on a path to it. What she feared was that women who slid into their late twenties without betrothal were screwed in a way they didn't want. It wasn't simply that they were afraid of losing their looks (though that was an issue), or that their biological clocks were ticking away. The scary part was, and she knew this from her own experience, that there was no good venue for meeting a guy once college was finished, because the bar culture wasn't there yet and "good" girls didn't have their own apartments and weren't living with a man, at least not if your name was Stein (Jewish) and you didn't want your mother to roll over in her grave. To put her predicament plainly, she was a 23-year old single virgin, living with her father and commuting to graduate school where she read nineteenth century literature that felt no more retro than her own barren existence.

"Madame Bovary," he said, answering her question.

"Have you gotten to the part where they ride all day in the carriage with the shades down?" she asked, a scene so famously suggestive that it had somehow come tumbling out of her mouth. Her face turned bright red.

"I guess I'm not there, yet," he said, though he was.

She looked relieved.

"But now I might skim ahead, you've made it sound so interesting."

She laughed, redistributing the blood in her face to the remainder of her body.

"C'mon," he said, thinking of a burger joint within a distance he could walk. "Let's get some chow. You'll bring me current on your family."

He delayed calling his mother until he had been out of the hospital a full week. He was concerned he'd have a relapse or that his parents would intervene and stop him from going on to San Francisco. And when he finally did call, it was strange.

"Harold! Harold!" his mother kept wailing though she hadn't called him that since he had decided in fifth grade he liked "Hal."

"Why did you do this to me?" She was crying. And for that moment he felt unworthy. Until she went on and on as she always did, and he got that old feeling that this was about her, as usual, and not him, his resentment percolating, his anger about Grovener, and losing his friends and all the other things he held against her.

By the time their conversation ended, she had made the usual apologies and promises to do better. And then the moment she hung up, she called Mortimer (the divorce had been finalized) who was teaching that summer at the University of Chicago.

"That little twit!" he exclaimed. "That selfish, inconsiderate twit! I ought to teach him a lesson and tell the Ithaca police department to bill him for their time! I mean it!" And when she told him where Hal was, at a Doctor Carole Chin's apartment, and gave him the address, he exploded.

"I'll be goddamned fit to be tied! That's two blocks from my place. And that's where he's been? Right under my nose! I'm going there now."

He hung up and stomped over to the Chin apartment, though the only person who was there was Elaine, who informed him that Hal was out buying snacks at a convenience store, and then shocked him with information of an infinitely greater magnitude, that Hal had been in the hospital all summer and was convalescing here.

"Well," he muttered, struggling to keep his composure, "I mean, I had no idea. Our family is not usually in such disarray, Dr. Chin. The divorce has made communications between my ex-wife and me imperfect, certainly, but that doesn't mean we don't consult with each other about our son. This has taken a lot out of us, Dr. Chin, not hearing from him. I would hope this kind of thing would never happen to you."

"I don't want to interrupt," she said softly, "but Carole Chin is my friend. I'm...I'm Elaine Stein. You know my brother, I believe, Michael Stein."

And indeed he did, Hal's roommate whom he remembered as so respectful and admiring, and so drawn to philosophy. And now this sister of his, a more fetching likeness of her brother, He was aglow, imagining he enjoyed her admiration as well, though in truth she was thinking the mother must be beautiful, with a son so much handsomer than his father.

"Hal will be back in a few minutes, Professor Hartfield. Won't you wait?"

It's not clear what broke the spell, though being called "Professor" was not what he had in mind. The sound of *Dr. Hartfield* could be music to his ears, but that was from his students, and this young admirer was not one of those. His disappointment was instant.

"I think I'm out of here!" he said, sounding no older than his students. "Tell my son to call me when he gets a chance."

He pivoted and headed down the stairs to the building's vestibule, Elaine remaining on the landing for the moment, curious as to whether he might bump into his son. But that didn't happen and, as Hartfield walked below from the base of the stairs to the entrance, he glanced up to where they had been standing, which further annoyed him because Elaine wasn't there.

———————

Mortimer Hartfield got an early start in life cultivating pretense. His father had been a traveling salesman, a Willie Loman kind of guy (without the smile or the shoeshine) whose wife died in childbirth, and Mortimer had the misfortune of being that child. In his father's mind and in his own as well, he had a debt to pay so that his mother's life would not have been lost in vain. He had to be important, powerful, rich or brilliant and, no doubt, at times fancied himself to be all of the above.

When he was ten his father remarried, an odd duck of a woman who had a few fertile years left, and they had a quick couple of kids together. The more Mortimer stayed out of her way, the better. He buried himself in his studies, wouldn't pick his head up from the books he was reading because his stepmother might assign him some house-work. And thus good study habits never had to be forced on him; they protected the quality of his life.

With his diligent ways, he was a favorite among the teachers. They would ask him to stay after school on special projects, and he was happy to do that, happy to be there at school rather than at home. At a young age, 17, he was admitted to Harvard on a full scholarship. Without question, a gifted student, but with some screwed up notions he had picked up from his father on how to live. 'It's just as easy to fall in love with a rich girl as a poor one' was one of his father's aphorisms. And taking it to heart, he married a rich one, the railway magnate, Rupert Harrison's only child whom he had met at a mixer the day before college began. Fresh from a finishing school overpopulated with dull girls from wealthy families, Margaret Harrison had been admitted to Radcliffe mainly on the strength of her family's donations.

By junior year they were married and Hal was born seven months later. Rupert was furious, blaming the pregnancy on Radcliffe's lack of supervision. In a letter to the president of the college, he railed that when he attended Harvard they had to sign in and sign out; *and they were guys!* On the Radcliffe campus where almost every student was potentially a pregnancy, what the hell were they thinking, he wanted to know, and demanded a satisfactory answer before he would fund a project the family had promised. The college replied, as tactfully as it could, that signing in and signing out hardly qualified as a method of contraception. And after Rupert had calmed down, he honored his pledge, though he would never pull out his checkbook for his son-in-law. He was convinced Mortimer was a gold-digger, that he had married Margaret for her money. On a couple of occasions, when his temper flared, he came right out and said it, that Mortimer would never get a penny. And that turned out to be true.

During the years he was married to Margaret, Mortimer made a point of clearing out of town for what he called the "accursed weeks" of the Christmas season. He despised the commercialism. As chairman of Columbia's philosophy department, he had the authority to decide what conferences he could attend, though it was difficult to find one in a desirable place during that holiday period. Margaret would go to Florida (with Hal when he was younger), staying at her family's Palm Beach home where the climate suited her insatiable desire for a suntan. She frequented a nearby spa where she sun-bathed even on cloudy days (using the tanning salon), and soaked in their vitamin-enriched hot-tubs before having her supple muscles rendered even more supple by a Swiss trained masseuse.

It's puzzling why Hal, in that first year of college, bothered to come home for Christmas, having just been there with Michael for Thanksgiving and knowing, from Christmases past, that the apartment would be deserted? Why *did* he do it, and given his unsatisfying relationship with his parents, why did he care if they were or weren't there? Because it was insulting, that's why, and he refused to accept as normal that they didn't care and weren't there. Call it contradictory or even delusional, he had come home.

"Not even a bottle of milk!" he exclaimed, holding the refrigerator door open as if to absorb the hostility of its emptiness, the omission of this staple his doctor had recommended for his ulcer.

He searched every part of the big, white box, which was easy because there was nothing in there except a few moldy vegetables in a lower bin. Was the cook fleeing a fire, he wondered sardonically? And why was the freezer bare as well?

"Goddamn!" he erupted, flinging a rotten tomato into the sink.

He couldn't remember a single thing in the four years he was at Grovener that his mother had done to acknowledge his homecoming, let alone make it special. A favorite meal. Some nuts or cheese. His coffee ice cream. Some little sign that his coming home was of importance. That was the part that cut to the quick.

He walked through the apartment to survey his options, a tour that only heightened his sense of alienation. There were paintings and wall-hangings he hadn't seen (she had time for the galleries) and, in his own room, clothes from as far back as grade school, and photos, wrenchingly enough, of friends he used to have in sixth, seventh and eighth grades; none of whom were friends anymore since he had transferred to Grovener. That was the shittiest part, he stewed, that he had lost those friends. And while he had never wanted to be one of those kids who blamed everything on his parents...he blamed them.

He grabbed his jacket and took the elevator down. And now, standing outside the front of their building on Park Avenue, he could breathe more deeply. It was a relief to be outside, he reflected, as he walked toward the theatre district, his hands behind his back, the way his father would pace when he was thinking. When he got to Broadway he found it deserted except for a few tourists trawling the box offices for tickets. And now feeling a slight rain, he hurried to a bar he thought inviting enough to enter, while checking his wallet to make sure he had his ID.

"I'll have a Screwdriver!" he told the hostess who seated him at a window. He watched people walk briskly by, trying to escape the drizzle. He couldn't help but compare them to the Cornell kids who, with their long, limber legs, young and laughing and even reading as they walked, moved faster than these people, and yet never seemed to hurry. This was just one of his thoughts as he sat there drinking his vodka and orange juice that took about two seconds to give him a buzz at 3:00 in the afternoon.

"Is there a phone around here?" he asked a waiter.

"It's out there." The man pointed to a red phone booth across the street.

He looked out the window. It had been there the whole time, of course, but he hadn't noticed. And now he thought of Michael and the things they talked about before drifting off to sleep—Michael's aunt and the Count, Michael's father who had dropped out of school to save the plumbing business, and the other family stories Michael had told. That was friendship, and as he felt a wave of self-pity, alone in New York without a friend, he downed the rest of his drink and scurried across the street in what, by then, had become a real rain. He slammed shut the squeaky, jerky folding door of the phone booth, felt the wet of the seat soak through his khakis, deposited the noisy, cascading dime and hoped Michael was there. He was, and the rest we know.

Book Three
Reunion

17

IN THE DEPTHS of the Depression, when Sam Stein dropped out of college to join his father in the business, Stein & Sons was failing, one step away from closing its doors. It's not as if young Sam was a likely savior, being all of twenty years old and without any business experience. But he had a simple idea that would turn the company around. In that grossly depressed economy when there was no new construction, maintenance of existing structures and facilities was more important than ever. Under Sam's leadership, Stein & Sons would reinvent itself as a residential services company and have more maintenance and repair work than they could handle. It was this simple idea that had enabled them to more than survive; to thrive!

"Are you going to want some help?" Sam's brother Max asked. He had just graduated high school. In these two years that had passed since Sam had taken over, the company had rebounded, with the commercial side now resurgent as well.

"You should go to college." Sam looked at Max sternly,

assuming a patriarchal role Max didn't concede.

"You've done okay without it." Max never felt the joy Sam did in learning. School was a means to an end, and he was at the end as far as he was concerned.

"Times are changing, Max. You know I would have continued if I could have. I didn't have that option, but you do. I want you to go on with your education. Consider the cost covered for the full four years."

So Max went to college for the next four years, though given his mediocre grades, professional or graduate school would not be a realistic option. Two months after he graduated, he asked Sam essentially the same question he had asked four years before: "Do you have room at the company for me?"

Max had been job hunting and hadn't landed a single interview. He wasn't panicked. To the contrary, at his brother and sister-in-law's place on this particular evening he felt the comfort and security of family. As he surveyed the plush furniture of Sam's living room where they were sitting, the request he had just made felt very reasonable to him. But that's not how it struck Sam who believed, that but for him and the sacrifice of his own college education, there would have been no plumbing supplies business and no college degree for Max.

"I can make room for a while," Sam replied. "You're my brother, but there are some things you should know."

Max rearranged himself in the chair, crossing and uncrossing his legs awkwardly as if they didn't belong to him.

"This is not the family business Pa had. That business is gone. It was so deeply in debt when I took it over, the first thing I did was reorganize it, what the lawyers call a composition of creditors. It was not technically a bankruptcy, but the reality was that the old company went under, and going forward it was a different entity. All the stock is in my name. That's how Pa wanted it. No assurances I could give him could chase away his dread of the Depression and his fear of lawsuits. And he was gone, you know, less than a year after the company was reorganized."

Max looked around the room as if to check the exits.

"Max, I know it feels like I've got a lot. But you've been a student in school and that's a whole other life. Take my word for it, it's a quick turn of the wheel, and you'll be where I am. So, like I said, I'm glad to have you on board for a while. I just wanted you to know...."

There were no more exits to check out. It was perfectly clear, as far as Max had it figured, that he had been suckered into a college education—a dream of Sam's, not his—that couldn't even get him a job interview, while his brother, as he had suspected, had those four long years to cement his hold on their father's business.

"You just wanted me to know it was your company!" Max finished Sam's sentence. He was walking out.

He left Chicago the next day and, after some months of meandering, settled in Texas where he married and had a son, Phillip. Except for a few business trips over the years, he didn't come back to Chicago. And he and Sam never spoke again.

"I don't have an answer for it," Sam would tell Michael and Elaine when they would ask why they never saw this other branch of the family.

"I've always regretted that," he'd say. "But it all happened so fast. Max was the first Stein to graduate college and then he couldn't find employment. There were jobs, but he hadn't gotten a college degree to become a construction worker. It was all a huge letdown. So when I opened my big mouth, he was at his most vulnerable. You know, when we were kids we could talk about anything and if we argued, even fought, the next morning was a new day and we were the best of friends again. But this time it was different. He was gone...forever!

When Sam got on this subject, you could see the pain on his face. It was a struggle to get the words out.

"He didn't suffer," he continued. "Your uncle Max has been very successful in his own right. I'm not going to say it's the college education I bought for him, but that didn't hurt in the circles he travels in. He's up there at the top of the heap. I know that from my suppliers. Everyone in our field knows Max Stein. He supplies bigger jobs than I do, some of the largest construction projects in the country.

"Look, we had a falling out and we weren't together, but there was still a Stein & Sons, the sons of Joe Stein. My father would have been proud."

18

MAX'S SON was a 23-year old genealogy student when he phoned Michael and Roberta at their home on a late Sunday morning.

"This is Phillip Stein," he said to Roberta before asking for Michael. It was then that Michael would learn that his Uncle Max was in failing health (he died the next year), circumstances that were life changing for Phillip, who was feeling the full weight of their family's isolation, an only child and the son of a mother who was an only child.

"I'm doing a family tree," he informed Michael. "And the more I've thought about the information I'm missing, the more it feels like there are parts of me that are missing. Our family rift, I guess you'd have to call it, is pretty strange."

"My sister and I have always felt that way too," Michael said, "that whatever happened then has nothing to do with now. It seemed beneath us to carry it on, like the Hatfields and McCoys."

"I know," Phillip said, laughing. "A bunch of hillbillies!"

And Michael laughed too, out of pure relief. "Just bring your papers with you," he urged Phillip, "whatever you've done so far. You'll stay with us and we'll go through it together. We've got a basement full of photos and letters. Hardly any, it happens, of my mother—I'll tell you about that—but lots of the Stein family."

Phillip came shortly after and stayed for two weeks, and in addition to the copious amounts of family information and memorabilia he'd sift through, he spent a lot of time with his newly found cousins, not only Michael and Roberta, but their son and daughter, Greg and Marti, all of whom would remain close with Phillip throughout their lives. Following Max's death that next year, Phillip would take over the business, but genealogy would continue to be a passion. And it was some twenty years later that he found Roberta at home to report, by phone, some surprising findings on the Harris side of the family.

Phil was adding a newborn to the family tree," she told Michael that evening, "and, apparently, with new software that he has, some Harrisons popped up."

"Who are they?"

"Michael. Do you not know any Harrisons?"

He stood there dumbly. This had come out of the blue. It was Friday, the end of an extremely busy week.

"Well, I do, yes, but no one related to us."

"Don't be so sure."

Roberta, you're speaking in riddles. What's this about?"

"According to Phillip, your mother was related to the Harrisons. He's going to double-check it, but he's pretty sure it's right."

"The Harrison family is Jewish?"

"He didn't say that. He said your grandparents on your mother's side were Jewish."

"Yes, I knew that."

"But your grandfather wasn't, originally; he was a Harrison. He shortened his name to Harris, changed it legally, not long before your mother was born. And if he hadn't done that, your mother would've been Ruth Harrison, not Ruth Harris."

"You gotta be kidding me?" Michael was stunned. "My mother didn't have enough money to go to college. And the Harrisons were millionaires many times over, when a million was a really big deal."

He looked around as if he were trying to find something. "Is Phil at home?"

"Don't call now. He said he'd call back before dinner. I told you he's double-checking."

———————

Phillip called at 6:00 p.m.

"Can this be true?" Michael exclaimed, tripping over his tongue with excitement.

"There was just one other database I had to look at and, yes, I'm sure of it now."

"This is going to be something weird, isn't it?" Michael asked. "I mean really arcane."

"Actually, it couldn't be more basic. It's all in the line. Your grandfather on your mother's side, Herman Harris, and Hal's great-grandfather, George Harrison (that's Rupert's father), were half brothers. They had the same father! But different—very different!—mothers, and that's what split the family. Let me explain."

"Okay, I'm braced."

"Cyrus Harrison founded the New York & Illinois Railroad at the beginning of the Civil War. Good time, 1861, for a railroad. Just moving the troops gave him a start. After the war his operations expanded westward with the acquisition of Colorado Rail and lines to the north and south between Chicago and California. By the end of the century, he had the most trackage under single ownership in the nation. But his capital was stretched to the breaking point and, in the very early 1900's he was saved by an infusion of money from Heinrich Moses, the scion of a well-known Jewish investment banking family.

"In 1908, Heinrich Moses's daughter, Dorothy, married Herman Harrison, the younger of Cyrus Harrison's two son's. Herman was 25 years younger than his brother, George. George's mother was Cyrus's first wife, Victoria. She died some years later in a Flu epidemic. Cyrus's second wife, Katherine, was Herman's mother. Like I said, Herman was a generation younger than George, but that didn't stop Katherine from wanting her son to rule the roost. The ambition and jealousy was intense, biblical in scale. When Cyrus died, there were miraculously (if you believe in miracles) some extra goodies for Herman and Dorothy, enough stock for Dorothy to give that young couple majority control of the railroad. A nice payback for the capital Dorothy's father had injected.

"George sued. He succeeded in proving undue influence by Katherine, and knocked out Dorothy's stock. The Heinrich Moses money was a loan and not equity, the court held, and it ordered that the loan be repaid to Dorothy as Heinrich's heir. That was done, and her stock certificates were cancelled. With Dorothy out of the picture, George had majority control and this was the key advantage that in the years to come, George would pass on to his son, Rupert.

"Herman, in disgust, redeemed his stock. The liquidity problems from the expansion westward had greatly reduced the valuation, and so George was able to get Herman's stock back at a bargain price. But Herman didn't care. He wanted to sever his ties, and left in a huff with Dorothy for Chicago. He converted to Judaism, changed his surname to Harris and, with the stock redemption proceeds, bought a large Victorian style home on the near south side two doors down from the Charles Comiskey family. Over the next twenty years, Herman and Dorothy lived off the repayment proceeds of the Heinrich Moses loan. But during that time, their home lost most of its value as the nearby downtown business district expanded. By the time Herman died (surviving Dorothy by a few years), he had so few assets his sole heir, his daughter, Ruth Stein, didn't probate an estate."

After they finished this conversation, Michael sat there, in a daze. So his college roommate first year, through a random room assignment, was family. What were the statistical chances of that? And when he had spent Thanksgiving with the Hartfields, he was with family, and when Margaret and Mortimer had hung out in his dorm room, that was family. As he had said to Phillip, this *was* weird, but in a different way than he could have imagined. The kids on the dorm floor used to say he and Hal looked like brothers, and he'd crack Hal up, saying "He's a member of the tribe."

"Well?" Roberta asked. She had returned from the grocery store. "What did Phillip say?"

He told her.

She wasn't surprised. She figured Phillip had gotten it

right. "Hal may be your cousin," she said, "but that doesn't make him a member of the tribe."

"You haven't heard all of it."

"Really?"

"Yes, really. He had a Jewish grandmother. Rupert's wife."

Roberta reflected for a moment. "Call Elaine!" she exclaimed, suddenly wondering about the effect of all this on her sister-in-law. It wasn't incest, she mused. There was no bloodline with Mortimer. And if you went back far enough, there were other cousins in the family who married, *first* cousins for that matter. But still—and at this, Roberta couldn't suppress a grin—it would be a shocker.

19

"I COULD HAVE gotten in the fraternity!" Hal said, excitedly. He was shouting into the phone.

He and Michael had been talking at some length, mostly about the Harris/Harrison rift. Rupert, had been so close-mouthed that, even as his grandson, Hal hadn't known about the Dorothy Moses stock claim, the lawsuit or anything else regarding Herman Harrison's estrangement and change of name. It was Michael who had dropped the bombshell.

"So you're telling me my grandmother, my Grandpa Rupert's wife, was Jewish?"

"Well," Michael said, his tone subdued but certain, "my cousin Phillip is one hell of a genealogist, and he's using a search firm that's the best in the business. That's all I can tell you. If he says she was Jewish, I'd bet money she was." He paused. "But let's wait for their report. They're in the process of confirming and writing it up now."

"I'd have to see that," said Hal, still dubious, "though I freely admit I knew very little about her. She was one of the best kept secrets in the family."

Rupert rarely made mention of his wife. Though he enjoyed the solid support of the Jewish community, it wasn't because that electorate thought he was one of them, that he had a Jewish wife. It was the feeling that Jews and a lot of other people had about Rupert, that he represented the upper class at its best (whatever that means), above the hateful spites, temptations and prejudices of those more needy and grasping.

"Like I said, I'm confident. But let me raise another subject—unrelated. I got an invitation today to my 50th Cornell reunion. How crazy is that?"

"It's crazy! But we shouldn't be surprised. It's basically a physics calculation. The closer we get to our final destination, the shorter the remaining interval. And for you and me, it's even worse. It's been more than fifty years. The more I think about it, that really is a long time. I've got to be there."

"How do you propose doing that? You didn't graduate."

"Didn't graduate?" Hal laughed. "You make it sound as if I had come close, even finished a year. But it won't be a problem. I'll call."

Though Michael should have had doubts, he didn't. To the contrary, he asked Hal if he would be comfortable with the traveling. "It's twice as far for you, you know, as it is for me."

"Michael, I'm flying. I'm not walking. And I can get on one of those old-peoples' carts at the airport if the gate is too far away."

"Well, okay!" Michael exclaimed. "When you call Cornell, tell them I won't come unless you do."

"I'm not sure that's the most compelling reason."

In truth, Hal had much more going for him than that. He had donated big money to the university, even by their standards, and it hadn't made a dent in his wealth. In the nearly four decades since Michael had been out to the house in Santa Monica, Hal had moved to a mansion in Beverly Hills and taken two more businesses public. And then there was the Harrison inheritance. Considering all that as well as the royalties from the renowned Hartfield Program, he was a multi-billionaire, no threat to Bill Gates or Warren Buffett, but somewhere on that list.

As he expected, Cornell was all over him, "honored to include him," they wrote, "as their valued guest." Which put him, basically, in the same position as Michael and the other alumni from the class of '64—a guest. This campus, while it may have looked the same—the clock tower, quadrangles, bridges, hills, gorges, bells and dogs—no longer belonged to any of them. They may have been erstwhile dorm buddies, frat brothers and classmates. But that was history. Here in the present, the campus, as always, belonged to its current occupants—students and faculty— and Hal as well as the actual alumni were merely the clay of a public relations program designed to mold them for now and the years to come, as nostalgic and grateful *donors*.

————————

They had agreed to meet at 2:00 p.m. at the Student Union, Willard Straight Hall (which everyone there called The Straight). Michael arrived a half-hour early, plopped into a soft chair, flipped through a magazine for a minute and then, contrary to anything he had ever done during his student years, fell asleep in the chair.

"Huh?"

He was awakened by a man, holding a cane, who had a hand on his arm. Somewhere in the gray hair, wrinkles and thick bifocals was the face Michael had last seen some forty years before. And so he popped up from his chair and embraced Hal, patting his back as he spoke excitedly.

"Why you old coot, you!" he exclaimed, and though he had wanted those words back as soon as they were out of his mouth, he hadn't offended Hal. Indeed Hal was looking at Michael with fondness, pleased, apparently, that he had been able to do this.

"You didn't think I'd make it, did you?" he asked.

"That's not true. I was confident you would."

Which wasn't true because Michael was still trying to absorb the shock of seeing Hal, of fathoming this temporal abyss. They were in their early seventies now, but Hal looked older than that which made Michael reflect upon the reality of his own appearance.

It had become painful to see the photographic evidence, especially the close-ups (and those shots from the side or back—there was no good angle), the proof that he too was an old man with age spots, wrinkles, jowls, and a gobbler of a neck. Where the years had gone was the mystery, notwithstanding the physics calculation Hal had offered. It seemed like just yesterday that it was his father who was the old one, who would avoid night driving, watch his spending like a hawk, and not commit to dates too far in advance. Now he was that person on his last lap of this race called life. He'd pass the baton to his children and grandchildren, young surrogates who had many of his own traits, interests and values, but that couldn't calm him at night when he woke knowing his part of the relay was ending. And in the cold light of the next day, that fact was even more clear as he took his meds to thin his blood and lower its pressure, to unclog his arteries and lubricate his colon. The old athlete could still get it together, but with more aches and pains than ever, and all he could do was hope this wouldn't be the day they'd find him lying there by the side of the track.

"Did you have a hip replacement?" Michael asked. He had expected as much from comments Hal had made on the phone, though actually seeing the cane was a shocker.

"Two, the second just a month ago. I should be able to toss *this* in the garbage soon." He glared at the cane as if it weren't his.

Michael glanced around The Straight, searching for chairs, but didn't see two together that were unoccupied. He would have given him his, but that was awkward. They used to race up Libe Slope together.

They walked outside to find somewhere to sit, Michael slowing his pace to match Hal's. Though he had friends who had gone bionic—hips, knees, pacemakers, you name it—this was different. This was his freshman roommate. They made it to the base of a statue, Cornell's first President, Andrew Dickson White, where they sat, and looked around as if they were on an island. Michael noticed there was no pack of cigarettes in Hal's pocket. That was the young Hal, the indestructible one.

"This is *some* weather, isn't it?" Michael said. He hadn't expected this, the unease he felt. It belied their intimacy of years past, the calm and quiet of each other's presence, and that's what he longed to restore.

Hal challenged him with a stern look, as if to say he

hadn't come there to talk about the weather. "Tell me what Roberta's up to these days," he asked. "Doing another special?"

"She is, actually." She had been a newscaster, but was now doing documentaries. "It's on increasing the level of technological knowledge in our labor force, what we need to do to keep pace with China, India and others."

"You're a lucky guy, Michael, to have gotten it right... I mean, to have found someone like her...the first time around. Too many of us didn't." Hal was a big fan of Roberta's. He'd often ask to talk to her before he hung up with Michael.

"Luck is the word for it." Michael pointed to an area about a hundred feet across the quad, "You see that spot there. That's where we were standing when you blew me off and walked toward the bridge. Do you remember? That was the last time I saw you before you left."

Hal stared at the spot, trying to remember while Michael noticed, for the first time, a tiny hearing aid in his ear.

"If you say so."

"Really? You don't remember?"

"Not really, no. I remember every kid and every teacher in grade school...what row I sat in. But when it comes to my year here I can't remember anything except the times you and I spent together. Colette asks me why I give the kind of money I do to Cornell. 'You don't even remember the place,' she says. That's a bit of an overstatement. But my memory is certainly selective.

"I'm sure I won't recognize a single person in that dumb fraternity I chose. I wrote my doctoral thesis on memory, that the things we remember are the things that take root. And, believe me, nothing took root. I can't even remember what *I* was like in those days and, besides, I don't think I and whoever I was then would have anything in common."

In their phone calls, they'd cover the basics. So Michael knew that Hal's wife, Colette, was still teaching, and that his daughter, Zoe, was a screenwriter who lived with her husband and their young daughter not far from Hal and Colette. And Hal knew from Michael and Roberta what was going on with Greg and Marti and the grandkids. So now that these two men had come all this way to be together, they could dive deeper to where the feelings were...like the guilt Michael felt about leaving Hal, as he put it, "high and dry" freshman year.

"No worries!" Hal responded. "I bet I spent more time and money than you working through that."

"And why would that be?"

"You're not being realistic, Michael. There was a whole other side to it."

"I hear what you're saying. But I just can't imagine it."

"Well, put yourself in my place. I was a loner for four years at prep school. Forget my role in that, and my mother's role, etcetera. Take it simply as a fact. If I loved being with you that year or partial year in college, that may have expressed the depths of my need more than the quality of our friendship. Putting it bluntly, you *could have been anyone* after my four years of torture at Grovener.

"Then let's focus on my negative views of the fraternity system; my conviction that it was an anachronism. There may have been a lot of truth to that, but it didn't change the reality that fraternities were the center of the social life at Cornell, that most of the campus leaders were drawn from there, and that's where a lot of the mentoring was going on. One thing we do know is that the kids in the dorms were marginalized. For most of them, that was not the ideal place to be.

So let's take a hard look at my decision-making. Fact is, that when it came down to the final hour, I joined a frat. I'm the one who decided that, and I picked a horrible one, not at all subtle in its shortcomings and with a pledge program that was truly perverse. I didn't have to stay there. It was so extreme I could've taken that fraternity to the school administration. I should have. I guess I wasn't as mature as I thought, and certainly didn't have the right, to impose my views on you."

"You're being too hard on yourself. You don't go to college to rat on your fraternity brothers. You would have become a pariah."

"Okay, I'll grant you that. So forget the administrators. But I should've de-pledged, simple as that. Like I said, it wasn't subtle; it was perverse. I knew from the first day— no, sooner, before I ever committed—that that fraternity was a disaster. But they were all over me and, like I'm saying, I was needier than I thought. A few of the seniors knew I was Rupert Harrison's grandson, and rolled out the red carpet. A real snow job! Once pledging started—I'm sure it wouldn't surprise you—I never saw those guys again. I don't think they were even active that last semester.

"When I look back on it, I didn't have to do any of that stuff. I still had a semester left living with you in the dorm, and plenty of time to think about my plans for after that. And if I didn't want to be in a fraternity or even stay there at Cornell, I could've transferred the next year to Wesleyan or Swarthmore. My father was tight with the presidents of both those colleges. Or I could've stayed at Cornell, been in an apartment with you the last couple of years. There was no shortage of options. If it was a drama, it was one of my own making."

"That would have been fun."

"What?" Hal asked.

"What you said...being in an apartment together. I lived in the frat house sophomore year, and then for junior and senior years I was in an apartment with four other guys, only one of them from the fraternity. That would have been fun...if you were there."

"So I got what I deserved. And right now I'm getting what I deserve. My butt is killing me!" Hal held the lower part of his back as he rose slowly. "What's your word for butt?"

"*Tush.*'" Michael remembered this was a word Hal knew, but not from him, from his Jewish friends in grade school.

"Yes, that's right. My *tush* is sore," he said. "Let's adjourn and get something to drink."

"Sounds good," Michael said, with great empathy. He was disturbed by Hal's grimace. That was real pain. Clearly he needed a more comfortable place to sit, and not just for a minute. "I'll be back in ten minutes!" Michael shouted, walking briskly away. "Just wait at the bridge and I'll get you there. And don't disappear! We don't have another fifty years."

———

Another? Where had those last fifty years gone? Unlike Hal, he had walked the straight and narrow. Finished college and law school in regulation time. An appellate clerkship followed by a prestigious law firm. An exclusive social and eating club. The weekend tennis game. Racquet ball, the lap pool. His own law firm. Business travel to oversee local counsel. Vacation travel with Roberta and the kids. An elite and enviable routine.

But was it? Had he forgotten how much he hated law school, the tension and the headaches? He and his fellow students striving to please some of the most arrogant professors in teaching. And then competing with each other for the scarcest, most prized jobs. The parochialism and homogeneity of the downtown clubs. The perfunctory nature of the business trips. And the return to the grind after the fun family vacations.

The sameness of it all! Chicago's Loop basically as it had been the previous generation—the law firms, courts, stock exchanges, clubs and restaurants. He'd walk those streets each day, to and from the train, and see the same people year after year, pace diminishing, waists widening, and briefcases thinning; men who could buy the same cigars in any lobby, and toss the ashes, stubs and butts on any street, sidewalk or curb.

Most of those buildings had been built in the '20s or before, a few still with elevator operators. And up in the offices, though there was new technology (surely a photocopy machine, slow as molasses), there were the staples of the previous era—the writing pads, pens and pencils, ink bottles, carbon paper and the other tools of a universe of hardcopy.

"Rose!"…"Mary!"…"Helen!"… Donna!"….

It was always a man calling a woman, likely his secretary who sat busily or often idly in a cubicle outside his office ready to hop to it at the sound of her name to take dictation, or bring him a file or coffee or anything else he might request. They were dressed to the nines, these cufflink-wearing, secretary-calling men with a window view *and a speaker phone, and while they might shed their suit jackets in the dog days of summer, never the ties. Though gone now were the seersucker, cufflinks, spittoons, typewriters, ink bottles, carbon paper, elevator operators, and dictation.*

Would you color that dark, those old office buildings and the dress code and customs? And if so, would you color the west coast light and bright with its casual dress and the oceanfront and the beach, and the palmy opulence of its suburban homes? That wouldn't describe Hal's life on the west coast in those early years. Nor would it retrace his steps from beleaguered dropout to successful entrepreneur. Because that path wasn't light or bright, Michael mused, as he kept a brisk pace to retrieve his car so that his former roommate, the hobbling Hal, wouldn't have to stand too long, waiting at the bridge.

20

THEY DROVE TO a pub where Johnny's Big Red Grill used to be. Michael had a beer; Hal, a coke, and feeling great relief from a cushioned seat.

"So I could've been anyone?" Michael said. "I think those were your words."

"Don't take it personally. I'm just being realistic about what my needs were and, I guess, yours as well. You needed my help in school."

"Saved my ass!"

"Then we're even, because you saved mine. Our friendship was a lifeline." He turned his head away, the profile so familiar to Michael. "Do you remember the kidnapping?"

"How could I forget it? I thought at first you were really kidnapped."

"I *was* in the sense that I didn't have anything to say about it, I mean, unless I de-pledged right then and there. They grabbed me and forced me into the car and started driving. These two jerks were from the city, and they wanted to visit their families. This was their idea of a joke, to take me along. I had one book I was carrying, on my way to the library to return it, when they grabbed me. That's all I had with me. Three hours later, they let me out at our apartment building on Park Avenue."

"Well, there go the kidnapping charges," Michael said. "Sounds to me like door-to-door service."

"Yeah, right...door to door. You remember, the building had a doorman who screened everyone. He knew me, of course, and so he let me go up. But I didn't have my key. So when I got off the elevator and went to the door—there were only two apartments on the floor, you'll remember—I knocked loudly, and heard mad scrambling. Our front door was thick, but I could hear almost everything. That's how frantic it was.

"'Don't answer *my* door!' I heard my mother scream. 'I'll get something on!' Then I heard a deep male voice, 'No need to freak out.'

"The elevator was still at our floor. I got back in and left. Better that than a scene with my mother standing there in a bathrobe pretending a man wasn't in the apartment. It turns out it was her slimy divorce lawyer. This was a guy who had no boundaries, none! Believe me, I know. I've seen his legal product. He specializes in false pleadings."

"I remember how bitter you were about the divorce proceedings."

"I don't remember what I said then but, yes, I was. During my last few weeks at Cornell, I was running back and forth to the city to attend those hearings. They were shocking. And the ironies didn't escape me. I was the one sent away to prep school right before I was to begin high school. Uprooted because of my sinful ways, which didn't amount to more than a sex education tutorial from our sexy little laundress. It wasn't that exciting, let me tell you, compared to the things alleged in my parents' divorce proceedings.

"If I'm to believe half of what was in those pleadings, my father had a girl in every port. Certainly in Scotland. That was his regular. He'd go there if he had a conference remotely relevant. He was the department chair and could put those expenses through. A great philosopher has to think about things, you know. All kinds of things."

"So your mother was, in effect, a single parent?"

"That's probably an overstatement. She wasn't home much herself. And so I was left to my own devices. That time I got in trouble with her and earned myself a four-year sentence at Grovener, she had been away on a trip. Have no idea where; she didn't work. Anyways, it was a day earlier than I expected her, and lo and behold, she gets treated to the sight of our laundress emerging from behind the closed door of my bedroom. My mother didn't think I was in there, and started calling for me. I still remember the expression on her face when I too came out of the room. Within 48 hours, I was enrolled at Grovener, Perkins, Pennsylvania, in the middle of nowhere. But at that late date, it was the only prep school of that caliber that still had an opening.

"I was pretty bitter about it, that I can tell you. I must have sent my mother fifty letters begging her to forgive me, to let me transfer to the high school where my friends were. After a while, I stopped writing...to either of them. I held them both responsible for the decision because the way I looked at it, either one had the power to get me out of there...and neither exercised it. In a way, actually, I blamed my father more. He should have empathized. He could talk a good game, you know that boys will be boys, that kind of thing, but when it came down to it, he consigned me to four years in a place I hated. Bottom line for me was, I didn't speak to my parents, either of them, and spoke very little to most of the kids; I'm talking about the ones at Grovener. I began with a single room because I had enrolled so belatedly. And then, by choice, I applied for a single the remaining three years as well. I wanted to have as little to do with any of it as I could."

"So you were coming out of hibernation when we first met as roommates."

"That's a way of putting it. I guess that's what I meant when I said you could've been *anyone* because I had cut myself off from *everyone*, and was most vulnerable when the fraternity rushing began. That first semester when you and I hung out was the happiest I had been since grade school. And then they were going to divide us because you were Jewish and I was gentile. Can you imagine anything more incomprehensible to the son of a philosophy professor who was an avowed atheist, and the grandson of a man the Jews of New York universally admired?

Michael thought of Roberta's experiences her freshman year at Michigan when she rushed a couple of the gentile sororities and attended their teas. She had been invited because her name was Field, the most legendary name in Chicago. But after the first or second time, there were no more invitations to the gentile houses. They had figured out in their catty hash sessions that she was a Jewish Field, not a Marshall Field. She cried that evening they skipped her room when the bids were passed out. But later, years later, she would realize those tears of hers should have been for the system, that awful system, and that she had been spared.

"Anyways," Hal said, "getting back to the kidnapping

fiasco...after I went downstairs I had nowhere to go. No money or checkbook, nothing! Of course in those days there were no ATM machines. So, with the jerks not coming back until 8:00 in the morning, I went to Central Park and sat down on a bench to think. And that's when I got the idea of going to the Cohens."

"Who were *they* again?"

"Joey Cohen was my best friend in grade school."

"Oh, yeah!" Now Michael knew who Hal was talking about because he remembered him saying that when he was about ten or eleven he wanted to change his name to Joey. And Michael would try to imagine Hal as a Joey.

"Joey's probably the one who taught you the word 'tush.'"

"Probably, yes! But getting back to my story, it was 3:00 in the afternoon and I was starved. I could have walked around Central Park for the afternoon but I would have gone crazy imagining Mrs. Cohen's food. So that's where I went. It was my luck they still lived there, because they moved three months later.

"I told her I drove in on the spur of the moment with a couple of my fraternity brothers and gave her a sob story about my mother not being home and the fact that I had no money or anything because we had left in such haste, etc. Whether or not she believed me, it really didn't matter. Mrs. Cohen never needed an incentive to help people. She emptied her refrigerator of every leftover she had, which was better than anyone else's freshly cooked food, and I ate for that day and the next while she and I talked, comparing my life at Grovener to Joey's experience at the public high school.

"Believe me, despite my putting Grovener in the best

light I could, it was no contest. Joey had a great experience in high school, and didn't need the added cachet of a prep school to get in the Ivy League. He went to Harvard, by the way. My whole visit with her was an eye opener."

He paused.

"I told Mrs. Cohen my frat brothers were picking me up that evening. I was too embarrassed to have her put me up for the night."

"Where did you sleep?" Michael asked.

"You mean, where did I sit and wait for my ride? On a bench outside Central Park, across the street from my mother's building. I didn't shut my eyes all night. I was too concerned about someone messing with me and, besides, if I weren't in that exact spot those jerks would've gone back to Ithaca without me.

"How's your father?" Michael asked, purposely changing the subject. "Is he retired?"

"No, he's still teaching."

"That's amazing. How old is he now?"

"He turned 90 this year. He's at a small college in northern California, Blake, where they're happy to have him. It's not Columbia. But it meets his needs. He loves the place."

"Reminds me of Hastings," Michael said. "They had all these legendary figures when I was in law school that were past their prime."

"You know, say what you will about my father, he's still an effective scholar. He's not publishing the way he used to, but he can still run circles around most people in the field. He loves philosophy, you know that. That's his lifeblood, more than anything in the world except Zoe and Mindy."

"Mindy?"

"Oh, that's Zoe's daughter. She's 4. Another only-child, and spoiled rotten, of course."

Michael smiled at the thought of Mortimer Hartfield, erstwhile womanizer and the sworn enemy of Rupert Harrison, now a sweet and doting grandfather and great-grandfather. "I sense your feelings about him have mellowed."

"My perspective has changed. I didn't like being lectured to. But a lot of that stuff stuck. In my graduate work, I found things he had said that I had stored away somewhere in my brain, things that were pretty brilliant. I call it the dinner table advantage. I had that."

"Do you see him, now that he's in your neck of the woods?"

"All the time! He wouldn't know what to do if he went too long without seeing his girls."

Hal's face broke into a broad smile. He pulled a large handkerchief from his back pocket and, held it in one hand, and then, it didn't escape Michael's notice, wiped it lightly across his nose the way his father used to do.

––––––––––

Michael would see Mortimer a year later in California and whether it was Zoe or Mindy or what, the nonagenarian had found the fountain of youth. He was still teaching and there seemed to be no end in sight. They talked philosophy, which was fun for Michael and, as Hal had reported, Mortimer was still awesome. There was nothing Michael could say or do that could more than scratch the surface of Mortimer's profound knowledge of the subject. Clearly, this small California college that Michael had never heard of must have been thrilled to have him.

It was a different universe from the legal profession, Michael reflected, which was all about clients, and got tougher in that respect with each passing year. After all, the old lawyers couldn't bond with the 30 and 35 year olds; not if the subject was zip lining or their kids in school. And as for the actual legal work, it was all right to use gramps' connections, but the work product itself was that of the younger lawyers whose unfulfilled ambitions kept the midnight oil burning.

For Mortimer Hartfield, however, the frame of reference even at his age was that of a thinker, a conceptualist. And why not? When most studies on aging indicated that except for the purely retentive powers, the mind, if not enfeebled by disease or disuse, continues to assimilate and interpret in an increasingly comprehensive way. As a scholarly professor, he could walk that small California campus like an Einstein at Princeton. And that held some real promise for an old man.

21

MICHAEL WAS ON his second beer, Hal his second coke.

"Why San Francisco? To be as far from New York as possible?"

"That, yes," Hal replied, "and the Horace Greeley in me. There's still something about it that feels newer and more promising."

Michael looked at him with admiration. Way back then, Hal had his own views on where and how to live, which is why they had argued about the fraternities. Hal never took his cues from others. It was years, Michael reflected, before he, himself, was so inner-directed, years of Roberta's influence, and the children and the law firm. It wasn't until much later that he would give real thought to where he *wanted* to live and what he *wanted* to do.

"I rented *Red River* a couple of weeks ago," Hal said. Now he was the one switching subjects. "Do you remember it? That must have been the late forties. Still a good film."

"Not surprised," Michael said. "Saw it when it came

out at one of the big theaters in downtown Chicago. Had a stage show, I remember. I was about eight or nine."

"Yes, it would have had an intermission—a long movie like that. The thing about those *big* westerns, the ones like Red River, was the perspective. They must have used a thousand head of cattle. And when they'd take the camera way up and you got a panorama, everything looked small against the mountains."

Hal paused.

"It's all perspective," he continued. "And that's why I'm going to transfer a portion of my estate to my father."

"Huh?" Michael grunted, surprised by this turn in the conversation

"Oh I know it's dumb from a tax standpoint, but I'm not talking about a large amount, not in relation to my total assets. Like I said, I'm grateful for the insights and analytical skills I got from him. They've been an important part of my business. He's not going to live forever. I want to do this for him."

Hal talked about it in greater detail. He wasn't looking for legal advice, and so Michael kept his questions to a minimum. Bottom line was that Mortimer Hartfield, with his modest Blake salary augmented only by his modest Social Security payments, could use a supplemental source of income.

"Believe me, I'm no hero," Hal said. "I wouldn't be here if it weren't for him."

This last sentence hung in the air.

"My mother was going to get an abortion!"

"My God!" Michael exclaimed. "We wouldn't be having this conversation!"

"I think about that a lot. And Mary had also wanted an abortion! There would have been no Zoe." His voice quavered.

Michael could hardly believe his ears with this coincidence that dwarfed all others. Hal had proposed marriage to his first wife, Mary, to save the baby—Zoe! Which is what his father, Mortimer, had done a generation before to bring *him* into the world.

"By all means, do it," Michael said, taking a deep breath. "I mean the transfer, if that's what you want to do. After all, this is not financial planning. This is from the heart." He leaned over and put his hands on Hal's shoulders. "It's good to be here, my friend. I've missed you."

———————

"As for my mother," Hal said, after feeling talked out about his father. "That's a whole nother thing."

"How long has she been gone?"

"About ten years, and I've gone through the full range of feelings in that time. Stage one was abandonment, because she was never around. Then hate, for her sending me to Grovener. And in the end, pity. I felt more sorry for her than anything else."

"Why?"

"Because she was pathetic. When you're young you don't think of a parent as pathetic. They have all the power. But by the time I was doing my graduate work in psychology, I saw her not just as a mother but as a daughter who couldn't live with what she felt she had done to *her* mother."

The waitress was hovering in an effort to turn that table over a little faster.

"Don't worry about her, Hal," Michael said. "We'll give her a nice tip. I'm not leaving now. In all the times, years back, when you and I talked in the dorm, I never heard a word about your mother's mother." He paused. "She's Jewish, I guess. That much we learned from Phillip."

"And I have some more on that," Hal replied. He cleared his throat.

"We called her Beth. She died the year before my Grandfather. That was my last year at Grovener. I wasn't informed of her death until after the funeral. It wasn't a real service. A minister at the care facility read a few psalms and then they buried her. That was how my grandfather wanted it. He and my mother were the only ones there. There was no eulogy...nothing.

"What happened was, when my mother was six years old, her mother took her to a state fair where the main attraction was a huge Ferris wheel that was left from, I think, the Columbian Exposition in Chicago. My mother put up a big fuss to go on it, though the minimum age requirement was eight. She was tall for her age, and so the Ferris wheel operator let her get on. Once they got underway, though, she freaked out, unprepared for the scale of it, for how high the chairs rose above the ground.

"Because of the noise of the motor right next to him, the operator didn't hear the commotion as my mother's chair rose to the top. She was screaming that she wanted to get out. Skinny as she was, she slipped out the other side of the restraining bar. Her mother, horrified, forced the whole bar open—which was either adrenalin or a defective restraining bar—and stood up to grab her daughter. She lost her balance and fell against the side of the giant wheel, her head hitting each spoke as it turned. By the time onlookers below alerted the Ferris wheel operator and he stopped the machine, my mother was screaming and holding on for dear life, while her mother lay there virtually brain-dead."

Michael was agape.

"It wasn't your ordinary Ferris wheel. It was the largest ever built in the U.S. and the third largest built anywhere. Because of its size, there were supposed to be two operators according to federal and state law governing the safe handling of machinery. My mother, at age 6, was a full two years below the minimum age requirement. And, like I said, the restraining bar was probably defective. In addition to those issues, there was the irony that my Grandpa Rupert was Chairman of the State Fair Commission."

"I never heard about any of this!" Michael said.

"You? *I* didn't know any of this until my *mother's* funeral when my father filled me in. Of course I knew my grandmother had been institutionalized for decades, but, like I said, we never talked about it. It was easier to deal with Aristotle, Hobbes and the others hundreds if not thousands of years away. And you know, in those days, the media was different. They'd blow the lid off things, like the Black Sox or the Teapot Dome scandal. There was plenty of yellow journalism. But If FDR was in a wheelchair or Joe Kennedy's daughter was having a lobotomy, you wouldn't know it until someone wrote a memoir a generation later. And so it was with my grandmother, whom Rupert slipped into a facility near the Adirondacks so she could be fed and bathed the remaining years of her life.

"As for my grandfather's political career, people wondered why he would lead the polls before every gubernatorial election but wouldn't make the run. Fact was, he was wary of taking it up too high, that the reservoir of support he enjoyed might melt away in the heat of the old charges of incompetence and lack of oversight."

"So your mother didn't have a mother either," Michael said, staring into the distance.

"No, and had her mother actually died, it would have been easier in a lot of ways on my grandfather. As it was, he still had a wife and that fact alone, at least in those days, was in the way of any other public companionship. So, his personal life revolved around his daughter, and her life around him. After he died, and she and my father had divorced, she spent most of her time at her father's old Palm Beach home. She was searching for a peace she never had as a child or a young mother. She took adult education classes and was a more diligent, engrossed student than she had been in finishing school or at Radcliffe. She'd read in the sun for hours by the pool, and got so dark she never noticed the melanoma on her back. By the time it was discovered a few years later, the doctors gave her six months to a year to live. As it turned out, she lived another two years, frantic the whole time about settling her financial affairs. In reality, there wasn't anything to settle. It was basically the life estate she had gotten from her father. And that automatically reverted to me."

"What was she so frantic about?"

"Trying to change it. The life estate had been created to prevent my father from getting any of it. And she hated that it ended up limiting her, that she couldn't prevent *me* from getting it. She'd rather have seen the money go to charity. She asked me to sign waivers and releases. I wouldn't, though I'm in the process of giving it all to charity now. I'm setting up a foundation."

"I'm lost. Why was she so anxious to prevent you from getting it?"

Hal drew his lips in tightly, one of his old expressions.

"How can I answer that question? When I left Cornell and didn't come back to New York or even tell them where I was, especially that summer I was in the hospital in Chicago, our relationship hit a new low. In my mother's eyes, I had crossed a line, though from *my* standpoint I was doing what I had to, to have a life. It wasn't until my mother was diagnosed with Cancer thirty years later that I knew the full extent of her resentment. I reached out to her then but it was too late. Her time was limited and she was more bitter than ever, convinced that any relationship we could still have would never make up for the years that were lost."

Michael glanced at the waitress who was losing faith that her tip could compensate for the lost use of the table.

"The story goes on. In consulting with her lawyers, my mother learned she could use the assets of the life estate to pay 'expenses of last illness and death.' So she decided to build a mausoleum. At first, when I found out how much money it cost, I thought she had found a way of getting back at me."

Michael smiled because there was no amount of money Margaret could have spent on a mausoleum that would have made a dent in the Rupert Harrison estate, and he said this, in so many words, to Hal.

"I know," Hal replied. "It wasn't the money. That wasn't the issue. I hate the place, the whole procedure. You have to get a key from the cemetery office to unlock it and once you're inside, it's so friggin creepy, I can't stay in there for more than a minute or two."

"I've wondered about those things," Michael said pensively. "Mausoleums, I mean."

―――――――

When he was a little boy and stood under his father's golf umbrella looking at the plants he and Elaine had placed on the grave, he had the comfort, at least, of knowing that if his mother was really dead and down there in the ground, she was still part of nature's grand plan—the grass, the trees, the birds, the sun and the rain. He was aware even then that, for some fancy people, there were small stone buildings at the cemetery with crypts in them and that these fancy people were put in the crypts. How awful this word, crypt, was, and how sad to be put in one. How cold and dark and away from nature. After all, even in the winter there was the fresh, white snow and at that young age he could never decide which was better—the sun or the snow. And his mother had both.

―――――――

"Well, you don't have to wonder," Hal said, "I can tell you, they're hideous, mausoleums! They're for rich people from families that don't visit the cemetery anyway because they've all fought so much over the money."

Michael laughed and, after a moment's delay, Hal laughed as well at the truth of what he had just said. But then he got serious.

"She built a second crypt in there. It's empty. It's reserved for me."

"You kidding?"

"I wish I was. A fucking crypt...just waiting for me as if I want to be buried with mommy. Like I don't have a wife and daughter and grandchild. Like I don't have a life."

They had sat there long enough, they decided, and threw some pretty big bills on the table for a couple of beers and cokes. It was quiet outside, the air cooling, beginning to feel like evening. Michael was processing what he had heard. So this was Margaret's revenge! If Hal wanted to relieve his guilt by visiting her grave, he'd have to confront the not so distant prospect of his own demise.

"It was my fault. I drove her to it," Hal said, as they headed back to the car. "I'm trying to move her out of there and wreck it but, so far, without success. Colette thinks I'm wasting my time."

He gazed into the distance. It was a stunning sunset.

"I was always studying when we were in college," Michael said, also looking at the sky. "I don't remember sunsets."

"That's probably right." Hal said. "Do you think I'm wasting my time?"

Michael's eyes darted back and forth, searching for the answer. On what theory could Hal have the mausoleum wrecked? It was the decedent's wishes that she be buried there, and she had made sufficient provision for its perpetual care. Forget that the second crypt, the empty one, was sadistic. That doesn't mean there's a legal solution.

"You know, I'm not an estate attorney, but my hunch is that your wife's advice is sound. I wouldn't try to change it. I would work around it."

Hal looked at him earnestly as if he had said something profound, though in truth Michael never felt so stumped when it came to giving advice.

"Takes me back to Red River," Hal said.

"How so?" Michael asked, still impressed a half-century

later by Hal's uncanny ability to integrate knowledge and information. When the young Hal was bored in his classes, he'd make lists of sports heroes, superheroes, authors, philosophers, scientists, other greats, and he'd integrate them. Michael thought it was nonsense at the time, a manifestation of the boredom. But years later when he reflected on the diversity of the people he had linked—like Nietzsche, Superman, Leopold Bloom, Lou Gehrig and G.B. Shaw—he thought it was brilliant, these connections.

"You remember the storyline. John Wayne was driving cattle down the Chisholm Trail, becoming more and more controlling, going off the deep end. Montgomery Clift, his foster son, took over and pushed him out of the roundup. Wayne caught up with him at the end of the trail."

"Don't remind me of the end. I'll rent it."

"I *have* to tell you," Hal replied, "because otherwise you won't understand what I'm talking about. You said 'work around it.' That's easier said than done. In Red River, the woman Clift loves and Wayne respects, intervenes to forge a peace between them. Who's going to do that for me? Who's going to intervene and bring *me* peace?"

Hal looked at Michael imploringly and then, mystically, read the answer in his face.

"Zoe?" he asked.

"I think so." Michael said, though the answer had hatched more in Hal's head than his. "When you visit your mother's crypt, take Zoe with you."

"And I'll know, when I look at that empty crypt that I'm not going there? Because I'm with Zoe? Is that what you mean?"

"Yes, and if you do that once, the empty crypt will have lost its power over you."

To Michael's surprise, Hal laughed, but this time out of relief. "They laugh at the end of Red River," he said, "John Wayne and Montgomery Clift."

"I told you, don't tell me the ending. I want to see it again." But Michael could already see it in his mind's eye—could picture Hal's family—his wife Colette, and their daughter, Zoe and her husband and daughter, all laughing.

———

When Ruth Stein realized her cancer was terminal, she was determined to leave evidence of her time on earth, and she began to knit. She had no experience knitting and was such a perfectionist that it went very slowly because she wanted every stitch to last forever. About a month before she died, she finished what she had knitted for Michael—a dark green scarf. He was too young at the time for a scarf and so it sat in his drawer until his first, big, adolescent growth spurt, after which he was never without it wrapped around his neck and drooping down his back, very artsy, his trademark through high school.

His good friends in high school knew the scarf's provenance and looked out for it on his behalf. On more than one occasion someone picked it up from a coat hook or a restaurant chair to return it to him. Though their manner may have been casual, he knew from the facial expression that they accepted their sacred mission. He took for granted this collective effort to secure the scarf, and maybe that's why he let his guard down.

A couple of days after Hal had dropped out of Cornell, Michael looked for his scarf and couldn't find it. He had just happened to think of it (it wasn't scarf season), though it was difficult to make an exhaustive search because, for part of that time, the Ithaca police had been in and out, sorting through Hal's belongings, directing him to leave everything as is. A couple of weeks later, as finals were coming to an end, he began to pack up his belongings and was free then, to search every nook and cranny of the room.

It wasn't there, though he remained hopeful. During those last couple of days he thought that every knock on his door, every ring of the phone was word of his missing scarf, though that was delusional. In reality no one cared. What in high school had been his trademark, had gone un-noticed on the Cornell campus where most of the students, sleep-deprived from studies, needed a jolt of caffeine to see where they were walking.

By the time he returned to Chicago he was glum, feeling that he had let the frat stuff distract him from helping Hal. Then add to that the lost scarf. He wanted to believe it was meant to be, that having completed his freshman year it was time to discard this security blanket. But, deep down, he knew that was a rationalization. It was the only thing his mother had made for him that had survived her demise, and now he had lost it.

Was it intentionally taken, he wondered, his suspicions narrowing on Zack Carter, Hal's "big brother" in the pledge program, who had hung around their room? The guy was always soused after dropping by Zinck's for a few beers, and full of cute comments, some worse than cute, down-right anti-Semitic in their denigration of his studiousness. Clearly, he was a low-life, but, more to the point, displayed an affinity for his belongings. He had come into the room one day to find the scarf wrapped around Carter's neck in a mock artistic flourish. He was outraged and shouted, "That's off limits, buddy!" And Carter removed it, though glowering at him as he handed it over.

Back in Chicago, he put aside his suspicions for the time being and hoped (irrationally) the scarf would be in one of the places where he had always kept it, as if it had made its way home like Lassie. After he had substantiated this was not the case, despair enveloped him more than ever. He thought of calling Zack Carter, and was in the process of looking up his home phone number when the doorbell rang.

It was a Special Delivery package. He looked at the address; it was from New York. The label had a "Mister" in front of the name, and so he thought in his confusion that it was meant for his father. Minutes later he came to the rather obvious conclusion that it was his name and that he was on the moral high-ground in ripping this package open, which is what he did in two seconds flat.

When he first pushed the tissue paper aside, it looked foreign to him, like it might not be his, or maybe was a substitute. These were the kinds of strange thoughts that crossed his mind for several seconds until his brain convinced his eyes to believe what they were seeing. Maybe its strangeness was also because it had been cleaned—all the old, sweaty creases were out—and by such a deluxe cleaners that it seemed new again, slightly sweet smelling, with the tissue paper not only on top but interleaved through the gentle folds of this perfectly resurrected talisman.

He looked at the mailing label on the package and, this time, recognized the sender's address as the Hartfield's apartment in Manhattan. There was a note taped to the tissue paper.

Dear Michael,

I found this at the bottom of the suitcase I had with me in Ithaca. It got grabbed up with the other clothes and hadn't noticed it until now. I know it isn't Hal's because it's handmade. If it's not yours and you don't want it, feel free to give it to charity.

Love,

Margaret

He removed the scarf from the box. The cobbled stitching of the wool felt more textured and intricate than ever, and softer than he had remembered it. The green seemed deeper, not darker but with more dimension like the leaves of a tree. He wrapped it around his neck and looked in the mirror. He was struck by the image, the resemblance to his mother, and by this scarf they were wearing that had been fashioned by her hands.

22

HAL WAS THE celebrity of the event, people wondering how they knew him—the voice, the eyes, the smile—some clues, but nothing solid; it had been 53 years since he had been their classmate, and for less than eight months. The alums who were in marketing and financial circles knew, for the most part, of the businesses he had created and sold, and knew that the Hartfield Program was the gold standard in its field. Because of his PhD, Hal had been referred to throughout the industry as Dr. Hartfield (yet another Dr. Hartfield), a title that furthered the program and the company as an integral part of the behavioral sciences. After only ten years in business, he had sold that company for fifty million dollars, approximately the sum his grandfather had left to his mother from a world famous railroad empire. And to make his bonanza even greater, he had reserved for life the right to all royalty payments from the computer age software programs it would spawn. By the end of this two-day reunion, Hal would morph from mystery guest to a Silicon Valley phenomenon who was viewed with greater fascination than anyone else who attended.

He must have collected a hundred business cards over that period of time, and only added to his aura by not having one to give in return.

Michael contrasted that with his own more ordinary standing. He was just another lawyer amidst a sea of lawyers, doctors and other professionals. Though his partners back home drank the Kool-Aid of the Stein firm's reputation, that was humdrum compared to an entrepreneurial rock star like Hal Hartfield. It wasn't surprising that plastic surgeons, hairdressers, manicurists, pedicurists and others were busy beautifying people for their reunions. These were the masks they wore to attend the ball. And if Hal's costume, in Michael's eyes, was that of an old gray-haired man swabbing his nose with an oversized handkerchief, the others there saw right past that to his wealth and spectacular business achievements.

What happened, Michael mused, to the cool, handsome, preppy, young fellow he met that first day of orientation who seemed so sophisticated for a college student. He didn't exist, of course, not *that* person. He may have had the ways and wardrobe, but the real Hal Hartfield was one of those persons who had a mother but needed mothering, who had a father but no father figure. Though Michael was preoccupied filling the gaps of his own life, his roommate had come to college with some huge missing pieces he would have to find and reassemble. And now after a reconstruction process of years, truly decades, here he was, the real Hal Hartfield.

"You knocked'em dead, big guy," Michael said.

He and Hal were in soft chairs at the Straight. They had just finished the farewell luncheon, the two of them staying till the bitter end, literally the bitter espresso that accompanied the dessert.

"I thought nobody would remember me," Hal said."

"Obviously they *wanted* to remember you whether they actually did or not."

"I guess that's right, Michael. What does that say about your classmates?"

"That they go where the action is, as people do everywhere. Your Hartfield program might instruct us that the secret to success is dropping out."

"Well, there are some great examples of that like Bill Gates and Steve Jobs." Hal paused. "Who was that guy who busted out first year, a couple of months before I left?"

"Overman."

"You know what? I actually remember that guy."

"That proves it," Michael said, "if *you* remember him. Proves that dropping out of college is the key to success."

"Or at least being memorable," Hal added, laughing at the silliness of it all.

They sat and talked this way for a while, lurching from the serious to the silly. It was fun. Most of the people at the reunion had left right after lunch to catch their planes. But Hal's and Michael's flights back weren't until the next morning. Hal suggested they have dinner down the hill in Ithaca at a steakhouse their classmates had been touting. And so they met there at 7:00 pm.

"I'm changing my whole life." Hal said, munching on crackers from the breadbasket. "I'm going to teach."

"Really? I shouldn't be surprised, but I can't think of another person I know who's changing careers at our age."

"You mean I'm on the late side."

Michael smiled. "Well, you're not early."

"Early is relative, Michael," Hal said, sounding exactly like Mortimer. "If I follow my father's example, I can teach for twenty years. I'm going to do some team-teaching with him at Blake this summer. Then in the fall, first semester, I'm going to have a course there I'm calling Philosophical Activism. It examines and analyzes concepts, but from the standpoint of their societal worth for this and future generations. The underlying assumption is that being a philosopher today is not sufficient. You must also be an activist. The future of our planet depends on it. So I'll be applying Socratic thinking and methodology to issues such as climate change, violence, the just distribution of goods, services and wealth, the polarization of our domestic politics, and the extremism of religion and nationality."

"Wow! That's an ambitious agenda."

"It is. We live on a tiny inter-dependent planet now, not the cloister Plato imagined in his Dialogues when he was debating happiness and democracy."

"Your plan to teach with your father is a great way of tuning up. I can tell you, of my own personal knowledge, he's inspirational. You remember that time I was in New York on a case and visited him."

"Not sure I do."

"What happened was, I saw him on a Sunday, thinking I was going to be wrapping up a case the next day on an agreed settlement. But the judge had an emergency hearing, and had to kick our conference over a day. So I spent that Monday going to your father's classes with him. To use the vernacular, it was awesome."

Hal looked proud. "I never did that. We didn't have that kind of relationship then."

"Well, you'll be team-teaching with him soon, but let

me tell you about this because it was quite an experience. We started with a freshman survey course where there were, maybe, three hundred students, all of whom were thrilled, laughing at every joke and humorous gesture of his, and participating from their lecture hall seats as he went up and down the aisles prodding them at random. Then we went to lunch where he was again surrounded by admiring students who wanted his attention and asked him questions. He responded with patience, and it was obvious from their reactions that they were accustomed to his availability. This same level of interaction carried through to a late afternoon seminar—all graduate students. There wasn't the more youthful adoration. That had given way to greater intensity, but they too, it was obvious, were in his thrall.

"By the time we went to dinner that evening, I couldn't get the sounds out of my head. It was like I had gone to a rock concert.

"How can you generate this kind of excitement, I asked him, each and every year?"

"That's my job, he told me, as if he weren't sure what I was asking. 'Man's ability to perform repetitive tasks is not peculiar to philosophy. You're a trial lawyer,' he said. 'Nothing's more steeped in tradition and sameness than courtroom procedure.'"

"Yes, I conceded, the procedure is the same, but the cases are all different, each with facts of their own."

"He changed the comparison. 'Is the surgeon bored,' he asked me, 'because it's just another kidney transplant? We hope not,' he said. 'In fact, if the surgeon has done hundreds of these operations, that's the one we want.' And I had to agree."

"Your father has the heart and soul of a teacher," Michael said.

"He is a great teacher. No question about that. I wish his personal life hadn't been such a mess. But then again, I wouldn't have had my sister." Hal winked coyly, knowing he had dropped a bombshell.

"Your *sister*?" Michael exclaimed.

"This is why I suggested dinner." Hal said."

"What's this? When did this happen?" Michael's jaw hung open.

"Five years ago."

"Mortimer fathered a child five years ago? Great sperm!"

"Now, Michael. Are you going to let me tell this story, or are you having fun just letting your imagination run loose? I'm into that, believe me, both imagination and sperm."

Michael smiled and held his hand out. "*Pro*-ceed!" he said, accenting the first syllable as they used to when they were freshmen.

"I was at a psychology conference in Pasadena on aging. That was around five years ago. It was a huge turnout and so the chances of meeting someone I knew were decent. But the chance of meeting someone I would learn was my sister was microscopic. What changed the odds was that, unlike me, she *looked* like my father...just like him! The resemblance was so strong that I went up to her at the first coffee break, and you could've called the paramedics, I was that shocked by what I learned.

"Elaine McDowell, 28, doing a residency at UCLA in gerontology. She had been born in Scotland. For the first twenty-two years of her life she thought her father was a man named James McDowell, who died when she was twenty. Turns out, he had this genetic defect and, after his death, when she wanted to explore whether she was also at risk, her mother confessed to her that he wasn't her biological father; that her biological father was a philosophy professor in the U.S. whom she had met at a symposium in Edinburgh."

"Oh my God! You don't say!" exclaimed Michael.

"I do say, yes. My father was in his sixties then. The woman was about thirty years younger—she's lovely, by the way—and is about sixty now. It happened that the timing of another, more dependable romance in her life was such that she juggled the dates a bit and attributed the paternity to that man, McDowell. It was plausible. And he was not so dissimilar in face and build.

"And that's how your sister found out? Bumping into you at that conference?"

"No, because I actually didn't say anything. I was too overwhelmed. We exchanged contact information and then two days later she was the one who called *me*. She had gotten the results she had been waiting for. They were DNA based; there was no disputing it. Besides, as I said, she was a double for my father."

Michael was in overload. He always remembered that, when he was a kid on the south side of Chicago, two sets of identical twins born at Michael Reese Hospital had been mixed at birth, and each didn't find his twin until twenty-five years later under a series of coincidences that were as unlikely as the original error.

"Colette and I drove to see her in Pasadena. We were there in an hour, and embraced. We were all crying our eyes out."

"Wow! You *were* going to tell me this all along, weren't you?"

"Yes, but I figured some restraint was in order. You waited fifty years to see your classmates again, and I didn't want my freak show to be a distraction."

"It's not a freak show," Michael said with real affection. "The most exciting thing is that you're not an only child. When I'd tell you things way back when about my family, I'd often skip my sister because you didn't have a sibling."

"But I have one now," Hal said, "Amy Armstrong—she took her husband's name—and she's pregnant and due in a couple of months! My father's as excited as she is about the baby. She doesn't really think of him as her father; more like a grandfather. But whatever, he's proud, he says, that she's the first real Dr. Hartfield."

"I thought you said her name was Armstrong."

"It is. At least my father has a sense of humor, in his old age, about the doctor thing."

Michael sighed. "Any more rabbits to pull out of your hat, or are you out of tricks?"

"Actually...I have another rabbit."

"What else?" Michael asked, chuckling with delight that there was more. Except for Hal and a couple of others, he had found the reunion boring. But Dr. Amy Armstrong, Hal's new, pregnant sister, that was juicy. He couldn't wait to tell Roberta.

"This is on your side of the family, call it the Harris-Harrison side," Hal said with relish, enjoying these drip-drop disclosures. "You're sure you don't want to have an after dinner drink?"

"I think I will," Michael said.

They ordered cognac, waited a few minutes for the waiter to bring it, clinked glasses and gulped some down.

"Okay," Michael said. "Let'r roll!"

"Well, this all happened shortly after our initial phone call about the reunion. The old Harrison home in Palm Beach was finally sold. The new owners were young and wanted a tennis court, which they decided to put in the spot where the guesthouse was located. But in clearing it out to be wrecked, they found, in a basement closet, a trunk with Jewish prayer books and tefillin. I had to learn what that was; I'm sure *you* know."

"I do, yes, but this was definitely Rupert Harrison's... this trunk?"

"Yes, because there were other things in there as well. Old photos of my grandmother, even an oil portrait. I did my own research, with a genealogist of course, and wound up substantiating your cousin's findings that she was born Jewish (her name was Beth, not Elizabeth as I thought at the time) and that Rupert had converted. The rabbi had kept that confidential. But the papers were in the trunk certifying to his studies and conversion. And while he never went to services, he wrapped tefillin each morning. Yet another reason not to run for governor...not in those days."

"My God! *Both* your Harrison grandparents were Jewish! I can't believe it. And Rupert was pretty orthodox apparently. It's unbelievable!"

"That makes him orthodox?" Hal asked, "wrapping tefillin?"

"Sort of, yes. I mean they're other things that go into it, but what's the difference? Either way you would have been killed a couple of times over in the Third Reich."

They were both quiet for a minute. It wasn't the casualness of the Holocaust reference. It was a matter of absorbing this information. Michael was the first to speak.

"You really saved a few surprises for me, didn't you? Well, like I told you on the phone, you could have gotten in the fraternity. And then you would have graduated in regulation time, married and been a poor schmoe like the rest of us. Instead, you dropped out of sight, led a down and out existence that steeled you to the rigors of life, and made yourself famous and a pile of money...."

"And I'm hobbling around waiting for you to bring the car."

"I'm not sure what the relevance of that is. Are you suggesting a correlation between drug addiction and bad hips?"

"This is fun," Hal said, grinning. "I'll miss it."

"You don't have to," Michael replied. "We have a guest room that's big enough for you and Colette. You might be slumming it a little, but consider the company."

"That's all I ever consider, my friend. The rest is fleeting...transitory. Like Stu Brin used to say *"Look on my Works, ye Mighty, and despair...."*

Always integrating, Michael mused, this boy-man quoting the philosophy professor quoting the poet. How miraculously he had reclaimed his life from those early years as a dropout and drug addict. The hell with bad hips! We can always get new ones.

"So it's your legal opinion," Hal asked, "that I can give my father the money? I mean, if you're telling me as a lawyer to do it, that it's good planning, then my father has got to accept it. It's not a handout."

"Well, now that you mention it," Michael said with the

kind of mischievous grin they would exchange when they were 18 years old, "it is very shrewd. You're involved in a lot of business deals that expose you to liability. And I can think of no better way to mitigate that risk than to spread your holdings and make your assets less accessible to creditors. I recommend you allocate portions of your estate to other family members, to your father for one."

Hal looked satisfied. "You really are a lawyer, aren't you?"

Michael's face clouded over. He would be leaving soon for the airport.

"We'll expect you and Colette in the next couple of months," he said. "If not at our house, someplace we can vacation together. We have to make up for lost time."

And then he thought of how old they were, and the half-century that had passed since he had graduated. Mortimer would say time is relative. Hal would say it moves faster as you near the end. Sam would have said time is money, and his mother would have said she never had enough of it, time, that is. While Hazel would have drawled, "I'll time you, Boy!"

He looked at Hal, at his face which had seemed so lined and saggy just the other morning when, at long last, they had reunited at The Straight. Hal had shed a great many years in these last thirty-six hours. He was more like the young Hal now than an old one. Which set Michael to thinking about perception and how subjective that is, because we control it. And with an inaudible sigh, he resolved that to the extent it was also within his control, he'd make up for lost time.

Epilogue

Mortimer Hartfield taught his last class at age 100. Hal taught with him for several years, and then pre-deceased his father. Zoe took her father's death very hard, and the fact that he didn't outlive his own father made her feel he hadn't had a long life. But really, it wasn't a short life, and in terms of accomplishments and the joy he had in the latter years, it was amazing. Zoe went on to get her PhD in English. She was another Dr. Hartfield by the time the film she wrote and produced, *Never Say No*, collected an Oscar and was a box office hit.

Michael left the practice of law after that 50th Cornell reunion, started a private equity and venture capital firm with his son Greg and, among their various investments, funded Zoe's film which more traditional equity sources had rejected. "It feels like an old shoot'm-up," one of them had emailed in shooting it down. And, with Red River in the back of his mind, that's when Michael committed the funds knowing Zoe had a winner.

Roberta, who had enjoyed strong name recognition

from her years as a TV newscaster, wrote a best-selling biography about the Harrisons, *Emperors All*. Though the Harrison's role in the New York & Illinois Railway was legendary, there had never been an in-depth story of its family members. The success of her book inspired their cousin Phillip Stein's book—*What's in a Name?*—not itself a big seller, but a very readable genealogy study based on the paradigm of the Harris/Harrison disunion. After retiring from the plumbing supplies and contracting business, Phillip and his family re-located to Chicago where he currently pursues genealogy to his heart's content. They reside in a rehabbed loft building that fifty years earlier was the downtown office and warehouse of a plumbing supplies firm, *Stein & Sons*.

About the Author

Robert J. Goldberg, educated at Cornell University and The University of Chicago Law School, was a founder of the Goldberg Kohn law firm in Chicago, and thereafter a founder of Bridge Investments, a private equity and venture capital firm where he is currently active as a Principal.

Reunion is his third novel. He published *Agent Only* in 2005 and *Jake* in 2013.

www.ingramcontent.com/pod-product-compliance
Lightning Source LLC
Chambersburg PA
CBHW032006170626
46807CB00006B/2673